PUFFIN BOOKS

Natasha's Will

Joan Lingard was born in Edinburgh, but grew up in Belfast where she lived until she was eighteen. She began writing when she was eleven, and has never wanted to be anything other than a writer. She is the author of more than twenty novels for young people and thirteen for adults. Joan Lingard has three grown-up daughters and five grand-children, and lives in Edinburgh with her Latvian/Canadian husband.

Joan Lingard

Natasha's Will

PUFFIN BOOKS

PUFFIN BOOKS

Published by the Penguin Group
Penguin Books Ltd, 80 Strand, London WC2R 0RL, England
Penguin Putnam Inc., 375 Hudson Street, New York, New York 10014, USA
Penguin Books Australia Ltd, 250 Camberwell Road, Camberwell, Victoria 3124, Australia
Penguin Books Canada Ltd, 10 Alcorn Avenue, Toronto, Ontario, Canada M4V 3B2
Penguin Books India (P) Ltd, 11 Community Centre, Panchsheel Park, New Delhi – 110 017, India
Penguin Books (NZ) Ltd, Cnr Rosedale and Airborne Roads, Albany, Auckland, New Zealand
Penguin Books (South Africa) (Pty) Ltd, 24 Sturdee Avenue, Rosebank 2196, South Africa

Penguin Books Ltd, Registered Offices: 80 Strand, London WC2R 0RL, England

www.penguin.com

First published 2000

10

Set in 12/13 pt Postscript Monotype Bembo
Typeset by Rowland Phototypesetting Ltd, Bury St Edmunds, Suffolk

Printed and Bound in England by Clays Ltd, St Ives plc

British Library Cataloguing in Publication Data
A CIP catalogue record for this book is available from the British Library

ISBN 0-141-30892-3

For Lindsey Fraser

AUTHOR'S NOTE

In 1917 St Petersburg was known as Petrograd, but in order to avoid confusion, I have named it St Petersburg throughout.

ONE

THE VISIT OF BORIS MALENKOV AND
MR HATTON-FLITCH

The day the black Mercedes came purring up the drive they had no idea that their lives were about to be blown apart.

'Mum!' yelled Sonya. 'Visitors!'

Her mother, Anna, had been bent over the carrots in the kitchen garden. Now she straightened her back and pushed her hair from her eyes with a grubby hand. 'B&Bs?' she queried hopefully.

'Possibly,' said Sonya, squinting into the sun. The car was long and sleekly black. The owner of such a car would be more likely to go to a posh hotel than to be looking for bed and breakfast in a family house. But one never knew. People were unpredictable, as her mother often said. And theirs was a very nice house, even though it might not be as grand as it once was.

'How many?' asked Anna. Her daughter's eyes were sharper than hers.

'Two, I think.' There didn't seem to be anyone on the back seat.

'Male and female?'

'No, two men.'

'Two men?'

Like her mother, Sonya hoped that they would be customers for their B&B. They were badly in need of the money. The bureau drawer was stuffed full of unpaid bills. Since Natasha's death three months ago, they'd been having a hard struggle to stay afloat. It was she who had paid most of the bills.

Her brother, Alex, who had also heard the car, emerged from the stable holding a bucket of horse feed. They had only one horse, Tobias, and he was getting on. Once there would have been half a dozen horses in the stable. Long before their time. When Natasha's husband, Alasdair, was alive.

The car pulled up in front of the house. Sonya ran across the lawn to meet it; Alex came from the stable. They reached the car simultaneously.

The two men climbed out. Their limbs seemed to be stiff, as if they had driven a long way. The driver twitched his shoulders and rubbed the small of his back. He was dressed in fawnish-brown tweed with a cap to match; his passenger wore a dark, pinstripe suit.

'Hi!' It was Sonya who greeted them. She was the one in the family always readiest to talk. Alex liked to stand back until he had summed people up.

'Good afternoon,' said the man in the pinstripe suit. He had a very smooth, even voice.

'Can I help you? Are you interested in our B&B?'

They had a notice on the gate at the foot of the drive, with a Scottish Tourist Board recommendation of three crowns. The men would have passed it. They were also featured in a booklet about bed and breakfast in the Highlands.

The tweedy one was surveying the landscape,

letting his eyes sweep down over the lawn to the loch. 'Nice situation,' he commented. He seemed to be speaking more to himself than to them.

'It's fantastic,' enthused Sonya. 'We love it. You can watch the sun set over the water on fine evenings. Two of our guest bedrooms look over the loch.'

But the man was no longer admiring the view. He had put his back to it and was scrutinizing the front of the house. It was a large, well-proportioned building in grey stone, dating back to the early part of the eighteenth century.

'Needs a bit of work doing to it,' his companion observed. 'The windowsills haven't been painted in a while. Guttering needs attention. Maybe even the roof. Been allowed to go rather, the whole place, I would imagine.'

'The old girl probably didn't bother about it much in her later years. She was ninety odd, you know.'

Sonya felt herself bristling. Had he meant Natasha? Who did he think he was to refer to her as 'the old girl'!

'It's a fine house, though,' said pinstripe. 'Excellent example of its era, I would say. A most desirable property.'

Property! That was the first note to strike a chill into their hearts. Brother and sister turned to look at each other. Alex's frown was black.

'Do you want to speak to our mother?' he asked.

'Or your father,' said tweedy.

Sonya looked up. 'Here comes our mother now,' she said. Anna would have taken time to wash her hands at the outside pump and tidy her hair. 'She's been in the vegetable garden,' Sonya went on, feeling

3

a need to fill the silence before their mother arrived to take over. 'We grow all our own vegetables organically.' She let her voice trail away. She had a feeling the men weren't interested in their organic vegetables.

Their mother was smiling as she approached. It would be the last time she would smile for some time.

'Good afternoon,' she said to the men. 'I'm Anna McKinnon.' She extended a clean hand.

The tweedy one took it. 'Boris Malenkov,' he said with a small nod of his head.

Boris Malenkov! That gave them their second jolt. Hadn't that been the surname of Natasha's cousin Kyril? She had lost touch with him many years ago. They'd never got on, she'd said, and they'd had some sort of row in the end.

'I am the son of Natasha's cousin Kyril Malenkov,' announced Boris, confirming their suspicions. He turned to his pinstriped companion. 'And this is Mr Hatton–Flitch, my legal adviser.'

Legal adviser?

Anna and Mr Hatton–Flitch shook hands and he declared himself delighted to meet her. For a moment, she was unable to find her voice, then she rallied to introduce the children, 'My son, Alex, and my daughter, Sonya.'

Boris gave them each a brief nod. They said nothing, but watched him carefully. He was eyeing Mr Hatton–Flitch, while giving a meaningful cough. He was clearly becoming impatient to get down to business. For business must be what had brought him and his pinstriped companion here. They had not come for the B&B or to admire the view over the Atlantic Ocean.

4

'How long have you been tenants here?' asked the lawyer.

'We're not tenants exactly,' said Anna.

'No?' He raised an eyebrow. 'So how –?' He let the question hang in the air.

'Shall we go inside?' suggested Anna.

'After you,' said Boris.

Anna led the way up the steps, through the open door, into the wide, spacious hall. 'Duncan!' she called.

The children's father appeared from the kitchen at the end of the hall. He manoeuvred his wheelchair deftly over the parquet floor, avoiding the elaborate curved legs of a mahogany armoire and the grandfather clock.

The two visitors looked taken aback at the sight of the chair, but they recovered quickly to participate in the introductions. In turn, each of the men bent their backs to shake Duncan's hand.

They then all went into the small sitting room to the right of the front door. This was their family room. Sonya wondered that her mother had not taken the visitors into the more formal drawing room. But perhaps she wanted to show the men that this was a *family* room. And a family house.

'Excuse the mess,' said Anna, lifting a pile of magazines from one chair, a book from another. A jigsaw, half done, lay on the hexagonal table in the window. 'Do sit down. Can we offer you anything? Tea, coffee, sherry?'

'A small sherry would be welcome,' said Mr Hatton-Flitch.

Alex fetched the sherry decanter and four small

crystal glasses from the dining room. He set them on the low coffee table in front of his father, who poured the drinks.

'Edinburgh crystal,' said Anna, noticing how Boris held his glass up against the light. She flicked her finger against the side of her own glass. It made a little pinging sound. 'Proof positive! The real thing. *Slainte!* That's "Cheers" in Gaelic,' she added. The glasses had been one of Natasha's many wedding presents.

They drank.

Boris made a rasping sound at the back of his throat, which he quickly turned back into another cough, putting his hand up to his mouth to cover it. Then he said, with a quick glance at Alex and Sonya, 'I wonder, perhaps, since we have business to discuss, if it might be better —'

'Alex and Sonya can stay and hear whatever it is you have to say,' said Duncan. 'We don't have secrets from them. Not many, at any rate!' he added with a smile.

'So you've not been tenants here?' prompted Mr Hatton–Flitch.

'We were friends of Natasha's,' said Anna.

'Ah, friends,' said the lawyer with a little smile.

'My grandmother and Natasha were friends from childhood. After Natasha's husband, Alasdair, died, my mother, who had just been widowed herself, came here to live with her.'

'As a companion?'

'To keep her company. But she was not paid to do so. As I said, there was a family connection. My mother was half-Russian. And then, eight years ago, when she died, we moved in to help take care of

6

Natasha. She had bad arthritis and couldn't look after herself.'

Mr Hatton-Flitch put the tips of his fingers together in steeple fashion. 'All this is news, of course, to Mr Malenkov. You must realize that he is her next-of-kin? And as far as we can ascertain, Mr and Mrs McKinnon, the late Mrs Natasha Fleming died intestate. That is, without leaving a will.'

'We understand what intestate means,' said Anna.

'Quite. Mr Malenkov, therefore, as her next-of-kin and only surviving relative, is her inheritor.'

The family was quiet. They had feared something like this might happen when they hadn't been able to find a will.

'Do you plan to put us out of our house?' asked Sonya.

'Now I wouldn't put it quite like that –'

'How would you put it?' said Duncan, his dark eyes on fire. His hands gripped the armrests of his chair.

'I am extremely sorry, Mr McKinnon, especially since –'

'Especially since I am confined to a wheelchair? Well, you can forget your sympathy! I don't need it. But my family do. My wife has known this house since she was a child. When Natasha was ill my wife nursed her and would not allow her to go into hospital.'

'I am sure we can offer you some compensation for that.'

'We don't want compensation. That does not interest us. We want to keep our home!'

'It's ours!' cried Sonya. 'Natasha said she was leaving

it to us. She told me she was! She put it in her will. She wanted us to live on here after her.'

'Where is the will then?' asked Mr Hatton–Flitch, turning his hands palms upward as if ready to receive it. His hands looked thin and dry. 'None has been registered. We have just come from the sheriff court where we have lodged Mr Malenkov's claim to the estate.'

TWO

THE MISSING WILL

They had searched the house for the will; they had looked in every cupboard and every drawer in every room. They had looked under the mattresses and under the carpets. Anna had even opened up the back of the grandfather clock.

'We were Natasha's family,' said Sonya. 'All she had. He wasn't!' She looked over at Boris. '*He* never even met her. Or came to her funeral.' At the remembrance of the funeral she burst into tears. Her mother put her arm round her.

'Mr Malenkov was not aware of his relative's decease until afterwards,' said the lawyer. 'A friend sent him a copy of the death notice in *The Scotsman*.' The notice had read: 'Natasha Fleming, née Denisova, late of St Petersburg and Paris.' Boris's friend must have recognized the family name of Denisov. It had been a prominent family in the old St Petersburg, before the Russian revolution of 1917.

'We will help you find other accommodation when the time comes,' said Boris. 'I'm very sorry, but I intend to go ahead and claim my inheritance. You couldn't expect me just to give it up to you?'

9

'No, I suppose we couldn't,' agreed Anna. 'That would be a lot to ask for.'

'Do you intend to live here yourself, Mr Malenkov?' Duncan asked the question politely, with no hint of the aggression he must be feeling.

'Well, no, that wouldn't be possible. I live in London. That is where my business interests lie.'

'We might be able to arrange a deal whereby you could purchase the house from Mr Malenkov,' said Mr Hatton-Flitch.

'We're not in the property-buying market, I'm afraid. We have no capital.' Duncan shrugged. 'Regrettably.' His accident three years back had left him unable to carry on with his occupation. He'd been a deep sea diver. He had been held partly responsible for the accident – he'd had flu and shouldn't have gone out at all, that had been his mistake – and so he had not received a very large amount in compensation. It was then that the family had started doing bed and breakfast, to help eke out their income. Natasha had had some money, enough to cover the expenses of the house, but not much more. And since her death that money had been frozen, on account of no will having been found. If only they could find the will!

Anna turned to Boris. 'Perhaps we could lease the house from you? If you could see your way to letting us have it for not too high a rent?'

His lawyer answered again for him. 'I'm afraid Mr Malenkov wishes to realize the capital. It is his right.'

'*Right?*' Alex spoke for the first time since they'd come into the room. 'What kind of right would it be evicting us? Against the wishes of Natasha?'

'It is a legal right, I'm afraid,' said Mr Hatton-Flitch

apologetically. 'And how do we know what the wishes of Mrs Fleming actually were? We only have your word . . .'

'Do you think we're lying then?' demanded Sonya. 'That we've made it up?'

'Sonya!' reproved her father quietly.

'I wonder,' said Mr Hatton-Flitch, rising to his feet, 'if you would mind if we took a look around? You see, we shall have to arrange for an estate agent to make an evaluation of the property and its contents.'

'Contents?' repeated Sonya.

'You must understand that if Mr Malenkov inherits, the contents of the house would also belong to him. Would you care to accompany us round the house, Mrs McKinnon? I think it might be best if you came with us on your own.'

'Well, Dad couldn't very well come, could he?' said Sonya.

'Hush, Sonya, that has nothing to do with it!' Her mother spoke sharply.

'Sorry,' she muttered. Her father hated to be pleaded for as a special case. Since his accident, he had been determined to lead as normal a life as possible. He did work at home on his computer, but of course he didn't earn as much as he had when he was diving. He didn't earn very much at all. Their mother was a skilled weaver and she earned a little money that way, but again, not an awful lot. So although their B&B trade was only seasonal, it was enough to make the difference and help them survive.

'Shall we start upstairs?' said Anna.

The two men followed her out of the room. Alex closed the door behind them.

'I'm beginning to wonder whether Natasha ever made a will,' said Duncan.

'I'm sure she did!' declared Sonya. 'She wouldn't have said so if she hadn't.' She had been especially close to Natasha and had been devastated when she'd died, even though Natasha had been in her nineties and Sonya knew that she'd lived a good and a long life. It had been a turbulent and dramatic life too, until she'd met Alasdair Fleming and he'd brought her to Scotland as his bride. In her last year she'd spent hours recalling it and telling Sonya her stories.

They heard footsteps overhead. The men must be with Anna in the upstairs drawing room.

'Will he be allowed to take everything?' asked Sonya sadly. 'All the pictures and the furniture? And the books? But a lot of the books are ours! And the pictures.'

'I'm sure your mother will point that out,' said Duncan.

'It's not even as if Boris needs any of it. I bet he's got loads of money. Look at his car!'

'Need doesn't come into it, I'm afraid, love,' said her father.

Sonya was unable to sit down while the men were overhead. Snooping about amongst their things! For, no matter what the law said, they were *theirs*. When they heard feet coming back down the stairs she went to the door and opened it.

The men were looking at the grandfather clock.

'That's a very nice piece,' murmured Mr Hatton-Flitch, making a note of it in his book. 'Swiss, isn't it?'

'Yes. Made in Zurich. Early eighteenth century, I

would think,' said Boris, lightly tapping the clock's face. 'Maybe even late seventeenth.'

'Armoire,' said Mr Hatton-Flitch, turning his attention to the next piece of furniture, a cupboard. 'Mahogany. Fine condition. She had an eye for a good antique, your cousin.'

'These antiques were all heirlooms from her husband's side of the family,' stressed Anna. 'They didn't come from St Petersburg.' Not much had come from St Petersburg. The family had fled with only what they could carry.

Mr Hatton-Flitch moved on to the pictures. He noted them down. Then they were ready to 'do' the sitting room. Their eyes did a quick assessment, seeking out items of value. They weren't going to bother with the twenty inch TV or the battered settee or the cheap hi-fi in the corner or the worn rug in front of the fireplace. However, Mr Hatton-Flitch's interest *was* taken by a sewing basket sitting on top of the sideboard.

'That looks a nice little item! It has a very Russian look to it. I would imagine it came from St Petersburg.'

The basket was elaborate, made of wicker and furbished with damask and satin. Small seed pearls rimmed its edges.

'That's mine!' cried Sonya.

'Natasha gave it to her,' added her father. 'For her twelfth birthday.'

The lawyer raised the lid. On the inside of it the word 'Natasha' was embroidered in pink silk, the colour now a little faded. 'How pretty,' he murmured. He took out some ribbons and set them aside. How

13

dare he poke around inside her box? Sonya felt rage building up inside her.

'Look at this, Boris!' Mr Hatton-Flitch held a small, silver thimble up to the light.

'That's mine too,' said Sonya. She wanted to go and snatch her thimble from his hand.

Boris had gone to look. The men's heads were bent over the little object. This was no ordinary thimble and it had never been used for sewing.

'It's encrusted with tiny rubies and pearls!' exclaimed Boris.

'Real rubies,' said Mr Hatton-Flitch, bringing the thimble up closer to his eyes. 'Valuable, I would think. I daresay it also came from St Petersburg. They made some very fine things there prior to the revolution.'

'Natasha gave it to Sonya as a christening present,' said Duncan.

'Do you have proof of that?' asked the lawyer. 'I mean, the basket is one thing. Worth a bit, probably, but the thimble must be worth a great deal more.'

'How could we have proof?' said Anna. 'Natasha is dead. She's the only one who could confirm it. Apart from the four of us. So I'm afraid you will have to take our word for it.'

Sonya was trembling. Surely they wouldn't be able to take the thimble! She prized that above everything else Natasha had given her, next to the sewing basket itself. Natasha herself had been given the thimble as a christening present. Her christening had sounded like something out of a fairy tale, with everyone bringing small, exquisite presents and gathering round the baby's white satin-lined crib. The Denisov family had lived in a palace overlooking the river Neva. Natasha's father had been a prince. That hadn't meant they'd been members of the royal family of the Tsar. Natasha had told them that there were quite a lot of princes in St Petersburg at that time. They had been members of the aristocracy, however, and they'd had numerous servants and kept two carriages. At the time of her birth in 1906, no one had foreseen the revolution that would sweep everything away and reduce the family to poverty.

'Of course I shall take your word.' Boris rewarded Anna with a smile which she did not return. He took the thimble from the lawyer, put it back in the basket and closed the lid. He then presented it to Sonya as if it was a gift from him to her.

Mr Hatton-Flitch carried on with his note-taking. The carpet was a bit too worn, he decided. Perhaps the family could make use of it? But the two Persian rugs, now they were rather attractive. Didn't Boris think so? Boris did. Finally, the lawyer's inventory was complete.

'That would seem to be everything in the house.' The lawyer replaced the cap on his fountain pen.

'What about the downstairs loo?' said Sonya, avoiding her mother's eye. 'We've got some quite nice lino on the floor.'

Mr Hatton-Flitch gave her a somewhat pitying look, as if she were throwing a tantrum. And, indeed, she wished she could stamp her foot on the floor and shout.

'Perhaps we might take a look at the garden and outbuildings?' said the lawyer. 'No need for you to come with us, Mrs McKinnon. We don't want to trouble you any further. We'll be able to manage on our own now.'

They left the room and Alex once again closed the door behind them.

'Do you think they're going to write down the number of spades we've got?' he said. 'And rakes? And I hope they don't miss the old wheelbarrow!'

From the window, they watched the men moving around the outbuildings and then crossing the grass to go down to the old boat shed at the edge of the loch.

'If only he would rent the house to us!' said Anna.

'He won't,' said Alex gloomily. 'He wants the money.'

'We'll find somewhere to go.' Duncan was trying to sound cheerful. 'Even if it's only a small cottage. The main thing is for us to be together.'

'But we couldn't take in B&B in a cottage,' objected Alex.

'And we love this house!' cried Sonya.

'I know, dear! But remember, Natasha survived much worse. She had to leave more than one home in her life and start again. So we can do it too.'

'We can't give in that easily though, can we?' asked Alex.

'I don't see what we can do to fight it,' said his father. 'We haven't got a leg to stand on legally.' They had already consulted their lawyer.

The two men were currently examining the boat shed, which was all but falling to bits. The lawyer was still scribbling in his notebook. Now he was putting it in his pocket.

'It looks like they've finished their stupid old inventory!' said Sonya.

The men were starting back for the house and their car.

'I'd better go and see them off the premises, I suppose,' said Anna.

Sonya and Alex accompanied her. They waited by the front steps until the men reached them.

'I think that's everything for now, Mrs McKinnon,' said Mr Hatton-Flitch. 'I'll be getting in touch with an estate agent and he'll make arrangements to call on you. And rest assured that if there is any way in which we might assist you . . .'

Sonya couldn't stand the man's talk any longer. Lawyer talk. Speak nicely and stick a knife in under your ribs at the same time. She turned her back on him and Cousin Boris and ran off across the grass to the old copper beech tree. It was her favourite tree in the garden. She loved its russety, mulberryish colour. She stood under its spreading branches and looked down at the loch. It was peaceful today, not a ruffle disturbed the surface of the blue-grey water. She couldn't *bear* to leave this place. She *couldn't*.

She glanced round. The men were shaking her mother's hand, pretending to be perfectly nice and reasonable. Surely she could reason with them! Plead with them! Ask them to let them keep their home.

They were getting into the long, sleek black car. The doors closed on either side, the engine purred into life. The car began to move slowly down the drive. The lawyer raised a white hand in farewell. In no more than one or two minutes they would be gone, heading south, back on the road to London. And her chance to make one last appeal to them would be gone.

Sonya made up her mind quickly. Taking to her heels, she went racing across the grass to cut them off at the entrance to the drive. She shouted and waved her arms in the air, but the car didn't slow. The driver was looking up ahead, getting ready to turn out of the gate, into the road.

'Stop!' she cried. 'Stop, *please*!'

'Sonya!' yelled Alex somewhere behind her. 'Get back, you silly idiot!'

Sonya didn't hear or if she did, she paid no attention. She went dashing on, into the path of the oncoming vehicle. It swerved to try to avoid her, but the drive was muddy and its wheels spun. The shiny black car struck her sideways on, throwing her up and over the bonnet. She landed on the other side, on her head.

THREE

SONYA IN A COMA

*E*veryone who witnessed the accident – Sonya's mother, Anna, her brother, Alex, the lawyer, Mr Hatton-Flitch – had to agree that it had not been the driver's fault. Not directly, at any rate, muttered Alex underneath his breath, but not loudly enough for the policeman taking down particulars to hear. Certainly not legally; there could be no dispute over that. Sonya had run into the path of the car. Mr Hatton-Flitch was able to testify that Mr Boris Malenkov had done everything in his power to avoid hitting her.

'He had no chance. None. She came out of nowhere. The first thing we knew, we felt a thud on the side of the car.' The lawyer smacked his closed fist against the palm of his other hand. 'Mr Malenkov is very distressed, as you might imagine.'

No one would deny that. Cousin Boris sat on the front steps of the house, holding his head between his hands. He looked as if he might be sick. His face was ashen. When they were ready to leave, Mr Hatton-Flitch had to take the wheel of the car, which now looked slightly less sleek with the dent in its right side.

Sonya was flown to a hospital in Glasgow by heli-copter, which came down on the lawn in front of the house to pick her up. Her mother went with her, leaving Alex and his father to look after each other. They watched numbly from the front steps as the machine went whirring up into the sky like a great black insect. They watched until they could no longer see or hear it.

'Dad,' started Alex, but he couldn't go on. He wanted to ask his father if Sonya would be all right, even though he knew his father couldn't possibly answer that.

'She'll get the best of attention where she's going,' said Duncan. 'Let's go inside, son, and have a cup of tea.'

Alex gave his father a push up the ramp to get him going, then followed him in. The whole thing seemed like a dream, it had happened so quickly. He couldn't quite take it in. He filled the kettle, not paying atten-tion until the water ran over. His mind had gone with his mother and sister.

To Anna, everything that was happening also had that unreal quality: the flight in the helicopter, as it swooped over glens and blue-grey lochs, snaking rivers and dark-green forests, grey-stone villages and cars that moved like child's toys on narrow roads. Then, as they travelled further south, towards the central belt of the country, the roads thickened with traffic, and houses ran together in long rows and there were factories and church spires and tall tenement blocks, their windows flashing in the late-afternoon sunshine. And all the time, Sonya lay like Sleeping Beauty on her narrow stretcher.

They reached Glasgow and the helicopter touched neatly down on the hospital forecourt.

While Sonya was being attended to, Anna sat in a small waiting room. From time to time she got up and opened the door and listened to the muted hospital noises: the swish of the nurses' soft soles on the corridor, lowered voices. After several hours, a nurse came to tell her that Sonya was in a side room and Anna could see her.

Perhaps Sonya would have recovered consciousness! A rush of hope surged through Anna as she followed the nurse along the corridor. But when she entered the room she saw that her daughter still lay with eyes closed, her lashes resting on her pallid cheeks. Tubes protruded from her in all directions. A large navy-blue bruise was flowering on her forehead, but there was no other visible sign of any injury to her head. Her pale, straw-coloured hair was wildly dishevelled and streaked with red that could only be blood.

Anna pulled a chair up close to the bed and took her daughter's limp hand in hers. She spoke softly to her. It was said that no one knew how much a person could hear or understand when they were unconscious. It was supposed to be good though to talk to them, to try to stimulate messages to the brain.

'You are Sonya,' her mother told her, 'and I am Anna, your mother, and I am here with you, watching over you. Dad and Alex are at home and they are thinking about you. We know that you are going to be all right, Sonya.'

A doctor came in. He said that it was impossible yet to estimate the extent of her injuries. She had broken a couple of ribs and had extensive bruising on one side, but it was the head injury that was causing them most concern.

After he had gone, Anna went to the payphone and rang home. She told them the little she had to tell. 'It's a case of waiting.' Waiting was the worst thing of all. Minutes crawled like hours when you were sitting in a small, hot room staring at a white bed and willing the person lying there to open her eyes. Just to open her eyes.

Duncan asked if he and Alex should come to Glasgow to give Anna support.

'It's too difficult,' she said. 'Where would you stay? You'd have to go to a B&B and that would cost money. And you'd have to find one that could take your chair. No, it would be far too complicated, Duncan. It's all right for me, I can stay in the hospital.' She would sleep beside Sonya and be there the moment she opened her eyes.

'If you're sure?' said Duncan.

'Let's wait and see how things go. Are you managing?'

'Very well. Don't worry about us.'

'I'm making Dad spag bol for supper,' said Alex, who was on the extension line. Spaghetti bolognaise was Duncan's favourite meal.

'Fantastic! I don't suppose I'll get anything as good here.'

When Anna put down the phone she burst suddenly into tears. A passing nurse stopped to ask if she was all right. She blew her nose and nodded, too choked up to speak. The reality of the situation had just overwhelmed her.

She took a few deep breaths to calm herself and then returned to her patient and the long, indefinite wait. People could stay in comas for days, weeks, even years. Sometimes they never came out. And if they did, their brains were often never the same again. She shook herself. Such thoughts would not do.

'You're going to be fine, Sonya,' she told her daughter again. 'You're going to wake up and say, "Hello, Mum. That was a big long sleep I had. And while I was sleeping I had the most wonderful dreams."'

FOUR

'*I*s she all right?'

'Look, her eyes are closed.'

'Is she breathing?'

'Watch, move her gently.'

'Careful! Mind her head' . . .

Natasha heard the voices as if through thick fog. She felt hands on her wrist, on her head, on her heart. Opening her eyes, she looked up into the rim of faces leaning over her. For a moment, they swam like photographic negatives in solution; then they settled. The night sky behind them was black, broken by a few floating white specks. Snow, she thought, gentle, dancing snow. Each flake looked a perfect prism. It was strange how everything seemed to stand out clearly, as if etched with a fine pen. In the past few days, fierce blizzards had been raging, causing chaos in the city.

Someone was holding a lantern. The faces flickered in its shadowy yellow light. They were the faces of strangers with bulbous eyes and mouths full of rotting teeth. The hot flow of their breath and the stench of their bodies enveloped her like a blanket. She felt a panic in her chest and tried to rise. Then she recognized the bulky fur-coated figure with the lantern. It was Pyotr, their coachman. She fell back.

'Are you all right, Miss?' he asked.

'What happened?'

'The carriage toppled over.'

The road had been clotted with thick ruts of snow. She remembered how the carriage had jolted and swayed before it had made that horrible, sickening lurch. She had screamed as she'd seen the road coming up to meet them. After that, blackness had descended.

She remembered something else too. Something that had happened before the lurch. The mob! There had been a mob, a crowd of angry men and women, who had come rushing towards them shouting, waving their arms above their heads. A young woman had carried a blue-faced baby in the crook of her shawl, but the rest of the band had been wielding sticks. One of them had thrown something. A cabbage, Natasha had thought. It had thudded against the side of the carriage. Pyotr had cracked his whip in the air and shouted to them to get back. But they had been in a frenzy and in no mind to retreat.

She looked at the people who surrounded her now. They had not been part of the mob, she felt sure of that. They didn't want to hurt her. They had no sticks in their hands. Their faces showed no anger, only dejection. The bitter wind ruffled their rags and their wild hair.

Pyotr told them to move, to give the young lady room to breathe. They edged away, as instructed, to allow him to set down the lantern and kneel beside the girl who lay slackly in the road.

'Can you sit up, do you think, Miss Natasha?' The coachman put his strong hands under her shoulders to help her. She cried out as a pain jabbed her chest. He lifted her up into his arms.

'Can one of you carry the lantern?' he asked. 'It's not far. Her family lives just along the embankment.'

Raised up above the ground, Natasha could see the coach sprawled on its side, its headlamps smashed. The horse seemed unhurt. He was pawing the ground and steam was issuing from his nostrils in white curls. There was no sign of the crowd that had attacked them. They must have vanished into the night.

'Bring the horse, would you, somebody!' said Pyotr.

Two men rushed forward to take hold of the halter. They argued for a moment over who should take it before one gave way. The horse tossed his head a couple of times and snorted, then came without further protest. The rest of the company trailed behind. Pyotr stepped out in front, the snow crunching under his knee-high boots.

Lights spilled from the windows on to the white pavement in front of them. The doors were all closed up. No one else was about. The wind off the frozen river was bitter.

They reached Natasha's house. Although it was a small palace – a palazzo – it formed part of a terrace and sat straight on to the pavement. A short flight of steps led up to the front door. Pyotr thumped heavily on the door with his gloved hand.

A voice was heard behind it. 'Who is there?' Not a soul in St Petersburg would open their door to a knock during times like these.

'It's me, Pyotr. I have Miss Natasha. She's been involved in an accident.'

There was a rattle of bolts and the door opened a sliver to reveal Stepan, the head steward. When he saw Pyotr with the girl in his arms, he widened the opening to allow them to enter. Glancing past them, he saw the crowd on the pavement and the two men in the road holding the horse. He looked alarmed.

'It's all right,' said Pyotr. 'They helped to pick us up. Can you ask Cook to fetch them some food and one of the other servants to come for the horse?'

'Go round to the back entrance in the street behind,' Stepan told the crowd. 'Wait there.'

He closed the door, fixing the bolts firmly back into place.

'What's going on?' demanded a voice. It belonged to Princess Olga, Natasha's grandmother.

'The carriage was involved in an accident, Madame,' said Stepan.

Princess Olga, on seeing Natasha in the coachman's arms, cried aloud, 'Tasha, my love, what has happened to you?'

'I'm fine, Grandmother,' said Natasha.

'You don't look fine! You're as pale as the fallen snow.' The princess liked to be dramatic both in her speech and actions. Now she wrung her plump hands. 'Carry her to her room, Pyotr! Call her parents, Stepan!'

Pyotr carried Natasha up the broad staircase to her room and laid her on the soft, wide bed. Her maid, Lena, closed the floor-length midnight-blue velvet curtains. The stove in the corner glowed with heat. Natasha let her head sink back into the pillow and

Lena came and removed her satin evening slippers and helped to ease her out of her shuba, her long fur coat. She seemed to have lost her fur hat. Perhaps one of the poor, ragged people had picked it up. She hoped so.

Her mother arrived with her grandmother puffing behind her. Princess Olga was immensely fat and puffed with the slightest exertion.

'I told you it was a mistake to let her go to that party, Eva,' she said to her daughter-in-law. 'The streets are not safe.'

'But she wanted to go, didn't you, darling?' Natasha's mother stroked her hair. 'And it was just along the embankment.'

'Those poor people, Mama! They were dressed in rags. They looked frozen!'

'Don't fuss, Tasha, my love. Lie still.' Princess Eva laid a hand against her daughter's throat. 'Where is your sapphire pendant, darling?'

Natasha put up her own hand and felt her neck to be bare. 'It must have dropped off.'

'Or been stolen!' said Princess Olga. 'That's the most likely explanation. By that mob. The thief must be apprehended.'

Neither Natasha nor her mother said anything. They knew the suggestion to be foolish.

'Prince Mikhail is here, Madame,' said Stepan from the doorway.

Natasha's father entered the room. 'Is she hurt?' he asked. He wore the brilliant blue uniform of the Cossacks. He formed part of the guard at the Tsar's palace fifteen miles south of St Petersburg. The Tsar was not currently in residence, being away at the

Front. Prince Mikhail was expecting to leave shortly to join him. In the meantime, he came home every few days to visit his family. He had had a difficult journey through the streets himself. His car – he had bought a Bugati just before the start of the World War in 1914 – had been surrounded by rioters at one point and his aide had been forced to jump out and draw his sword to clear the way. 'The mob attacked your coach, so I hear,' he said, pulling up a chair to Natasha's bedside.

'Father, one of the women had a baby in her arms. It might have been dead.'

'Hush now, darling.' Her mother leant over to lay a hand against her forehead. To her husband she said, 'She is a little feverish, Mikhail.'

'No wonder,' said Princess Olga, 'after such a dreadful experience.'

'It wasn't so dreadful,' said Natasha. 'The people who helped us were very kind. You'll reward them, Papa, won't you?'

'I already have.' He sat on the edge of the bed. He looked so handsome, her father, in his uniform. 'Do you ache anywhere?'

Natasha put her hand to her midriff. 'There,' she said.

'I think she may have damaged her ribs,' volunteered Pyotr.

'We must send for the doctor,' said Natasha's grandmother.

Pyotr was ordered to go and fetch him, but the doctor refused to come out. 'Tell them to bind up the child's ribs,' he said to the coachman. 'I am not going to risk my life coming out.'

The news, when Pyotr brought it, was not well received.

'This is outrageous!' said Prince Ivan, Natasha's grandfather, emerging from his study with a glass of ruby red wine in his hand. The colour of his face matched that of the wine. 'How dare the man refuse to come!' Such a thing had never happened before.

'There's a new order afoot, Father,' said Prince Mikhail.

'New order! It's sheer anarchy, nothing else. The Tsar will have to crush it and do it fast. The trouble is the man's too soft. No backbone.'

Natasha's maid began to bind up her ribs. She wound the bandages carefully, trying not to make the patient wince.

'Where do those poor people live, Lena?' asked Natasha.

'In doorways. Under bridges.'

'But why don't they freeze to death?'

'They often do. That is why there is going to be a revolution.'

FIVE

ALEX BEGINS A NEW SEARCH

Neighbours called on Alex and his father to offer help and sympathy. Mr Bell, the minister, said he would run them to Glasgow whenever they wanted to go. They just had to say the word. Duncan thanked him.

'But I think we'll leave it in the meantime. We'll wait.'

'Phone any time. Even in the middle of the night.'

They knew Mr Bell meant, in case Sonya's condition deteriorated.

The waiting was difficult for Alex and his father, just as it was for Anna in the hospital. Time, in the house by the loch, moved slowly and heavily. Alex found himself glancing at his watch every few minutes. Often the hands seemed not to have moved since he'd last looked. Usually he found that there weren't enough minutes in the day to do everything he wanted to do. Whenever the phone rang, his heart somersaulted and he would almost let the receiver drop through his fingers. His mother phoned three times a day.

'No change,' she'd say in an exhausted voice.

Alex and his father tried to stay optimistic and cheerful, but at times their spirits failed.

'We must try to keep busy,' said Duncan. 'It's a pity it's holiday time. It would be better for you if you were at school.'

'But then you'd be on your own all day!'

Alex was glad that he wasn't at school. He didn't know how he could have sat still at a desk and concentrated on maths or French. He preferred to be moving, preferably out in the fresh air, with the smell of the sea in his head. He roamed the loch shore in the early morning, unable to sleep once the light had started to seep into the sky and the land. He took Tobias for long, slow walks through the woods and talked to him as they went. He did their daily shopping at the small shop-cum-post office in the village, going in first thing in the morning on his bike.

'Any change?' asked Mrs Robertson as she put eggs into a box for him. That was what everyone asked. 'How many days is that now?'

'Four.'

'You're having a hard time of it at the moment, aren't you, lad? First, your dad. Then you hear you're to be put out your house. That's an absolute disgrace, that is! And now there's your poor sister.' She shook her head. 'They say bad luck comes in threes. You could be doing with a bit of good luck now.'

Alex agreed. Cycling home, he thought about that. His mother always said that you made your own luck, within reason. What a bit of luck it would be if they could find Natasha's will. If one existed. Sonya had been convinced that it did. She was sure it must be in the house, somewhere. In her last year, Natasha had become a little odd, the way some old people do, not too much, but a bit. She had started to hide things. 'Just to keep them safe,' she would say and smile mysteriously. She had always liked mysteries. And she'd loved hiding things and setting up treasure hunts. Once Sonya had asked her who she was keeping the things safe from and she'd said, 'Why, the Red Guard, of course! They'd take the skin off your back if they could. You know they murdered my grandfather?'

Sometimes she wouldn't be able to remember where she'd put whatever it was that she'd hidden and Anna would have to rummage through her drawers and try to find it for her.

So Natasha might have been forgetful and a bit fanciful but, in spite of that, she had remained sharp mentally. She had told Sonya that she'd put the will away carefully, where the Red Guard wouldn't find it. 'But you'll find it, I know you will. You're a smart girl. You'll figure it out.' Then she'd said something about a musket. But there were no muskets in the house!

'I'm going to search the house again!' Alex announced to his father when he came in with the shopping.

His eye was caught first by Sonya's sewing basket. He lifted the lid and took out each item: the ruby and pearl thimble; a set of needles in an unopened packet, made in Paris; a small pair of silver scissors; a silver-backed locket containing photographs of Natasha's mother on one side and her father on the other. There were hanks of silk thread too, in glowing colours: tangerine, emerald, turquoise, sunflower yellow and royal blue. Some of the colours had dimmed a little, but others were amazingly bright after so many years. He ran his fingers over the satin lining, turned the box on to each of its sides, then examined the back. There was no place here for a will to be hidden.

He went upstairs to Natasha's bedroom, which they had left as it was before her death. His mother had searched the room before. He felt funny being in Natasha's room, opening her cupboards, prying in her writing desk. For that was what it felt like: prying. Yet he felt he had no option. If he didn't, removal men would come and take everything away and any papers or personal objects would fall into the hands of Cousin Boris! The thought of that egged Alex on.

He removed every piece of paper from the desk. Some were just scraps, old bills, notes in Natasha's handwriting, but he read every word of each one, hoping for some clue. The rest were letters, written in ink now faded, and headed Paris, Berlin, Madrid and London, and dated from the forties onwards. In recent years the letters had become fewer as many of her old friends had died.

Alex turned his attention next to the mattress on the bed. Old people were supposed to think that a good place to hide things like money. Or perhaps wills? He went over every inch of the mattress. Nothing there.

He examined the pillows and took the covers off the chair cushions. Nothing.

He rolled back the carpet. He crawled over every metre of the floor underneath. The dust made him sneeze. There was nothing there but dust.

He went back downstairs to his father.

'Dad, can you remember exactly what Natasha is supposed to have said to Sonya?'

'Something about a musket.'

'Yes, I know that. But what else?'

'Didn't she say, "You'll find me there with a musket"?'

They had looked through all Natasha's old photographs to see, if by any strange chance, there was one of her with a musket that might give them a clue. But there had been none.

'When your mother phones we'll ask her if she remembers any more.'

Anna rang shortly afterwards.

'It didn't seem to make sense,' she agreed, 'what she said to Sonya. I think Natasha must have been quite confused at that stage. Also, she could be a bit of devil, as you know.'

'But she did *want* us to find the will,' said Alex.

'True.' Anna sighed. 'I believe on another occasion she said something about a white bird giving a clue to the will, or something to that effect.'

After the call, Alex and his father sat in the study brooding.

'A white bird,' said Duncan. 'What white birds do we know?'

'Seagulls.' There were always plenty of them on the loch shore. At times, they could be a menace, especially in the breeding season. Once Sonya had been attacked by one. 'Perhaps Natasha meant us to look near the sea.' Alex jumped up. 'I'm going to search the boat shed.' They had not thought of that as a hiding place before.

He ran down to the loch. A seagull was sitting on

the roof of the boat shed. That might be a good omen! Alex tugged open the door, which was inclined to stick. The shed was in a sorry mess. They had been meaning to clear it up for ages. Where to start? To tidy the place might be as good a way as any other.

He began by dragging out their old dinghy. Before setting it aside on the grass, he examined every inch, though he wasn't hopeful about finding anything there. For, after all, they still used it to potter about on the loch close to the shore and it wasn't very likely that Natasha would want to risk hiding a will somewhere it could get soaking wet. Come to think of it, it wasn't terribly likely she would choose the boat shed as a hiding place. But he carried on anyway. His search, if he was to pursue it at all, would have to be thorough.

Alex searched the shed minutely but found nothing. He returned to the house.

'We must try a different tack,' said Duncan. 'Let's think about other white birds.'

'Doves,' said Alex. 'They're white. But we don't have any.' The house over the hill had a 'doocot'. A dovecot. But Natasha wouldn't have gone over there.

'So then we have the word muskets,' mused Duncan. 'What does that suggest?'

'War.'

'And doves are a symbol of peace!' Duncan sat up straight. 'You'll find *me* there. Natasha!' he said excitedly. 'Natasha is the heroine in the famous Russian novel *War and Peace* by Tolstoy!'

SIX

ST PETERSBURG, FEBRUARY 1917
THE REVOLUTION COMES

*N*atasha was sewing. She had to do something. She couldn't concentrate to read. Everyone in the house was on edge. Trouble hung in the air like a bad smell. She hadn't been out since the night of her accident. Law and order had broken down completely in the streets. Even inside the closed-up building, with its sealed windows and bolted doors, they could hear the rioters. They were like prisoners in their own house, peering out of the long windows at the crowds gathered on the frozen river waving red banners.

Most of their servants had disappeared. The housemaids and the kitchen maids, the laundry maids and the porters and the little men called 'moujiks', who wore brightly coloured shirts and high boots, and swept the carpets, stoked the furnaces, washed dishes and slid on cloths over the floors to polish them. Natasha had never known exactly how many servants they had had, but at least two dozen.

'Where have they gone?' she asked Lena.

'Back to their villages in the country. They don't want to get caught up in the trouble.' Lena went out on forays into the streets and brought back news. 'Or else they've joined the rioters.'

'The moujiks?' Natasha couldn't imagine the little men rioting. They'd been friendly and had often sung as they'd gone about their duties.

In former times, the house had been full of bustle and noise. The doorbell had rung constantly. Her mother and grandmother had entertained in the salon, serving tea, in small decorated teapots, made with hot water from the pot-bellied copper samovar that steamed gently in a corner for most of the day. With it, they had offered cakes: gooey meringues, crisp little honey and almond cakes, chocolate profiteroles, coffee and walnut cake.

Now there were no cakes in the house. The shop on the Nevsky Boulevard was closed. The doorbell didn't ring. It was quiet and still in the hall and corridors. People spoke in lowered voices in case an enemy might be listening. For it seemed that there were thousands out there baying for their blood. The sound of their cries was terrifying.

The weather had continued to be severe, with temperatures dropping to as low as thirty degrees below zero. Schools were shut down due to shortage of fuel. Mostly everything in the city was closed: shops, factories. There was no public transport, no newspapers. Snow was piled up on the railway tracks; trains were stuck. Food was scarce. Lena said the peasants were refusing to bring produce into the city. It was thought bread would be rationed. People were becoming hungrier and angrier by the day. Police stations had been set alight and troops had opened fire. Some people had been killed.

'Why do they hate us so much, Lena?' asked Natasha.

The maid shrugged. 'When people are cold and hungry, Miss Natasha, they get angry.'

'But it's not our fault!'

'You've got more than they have, that's what makes them angry.'

Natasha followed Lena's gaze as it travelled round the room, taking in the furniture and rich upholstery. She began to see things through the maid's eyes, noticing, as though for the first time, the emerald-green velvet dress that lay on the sofa waiting for Lena to mend the hem and the scarlet fur-lined velvet cloak that hung on the back of the door. She loved wearing velvet in winter, and fur when she went outside. She wondered when she would be able to go outside again. Her grandfather said they were marked people. She shivered at the thought.

'Can't we give them something of ours?' asked Natasha. She would gladly part with some of her clothes. She had more than she needed.

'It's too late now,' said Lena, threading a needle with emerald green thread and taking up the dress.

Natasha wished she could run out into the snow and find the ragged woman with the baby and give her the scarlet cloak to keep them warm. But, as Lena said, it was too late now. The maid had a closed-up look on her face. Was she cross with them too?

'*You're* not going to leave us, are you, Lena? Please don't! What would I do if you went?'

'I dare say I shall stay, Miss Natasha. I have no great wish to go back to my village. It's a poor place. The houses are no more than hovels.' Lena had come from a remote village up north, before Natasha was born. 'I don't know what you'd all do without me, I'm sure.' They were coming to depend on her more and more. 'Ask Lena!' was the cry whenever anyone didn't know what to do.

They heard noise below. Lena opened the door and cocked her ear. 'It's just your grandfather having his bit of a rant. Poor old soul.'

Prince Ivan was the one person in the house who did not keep his voice down. He stomped around with his stick, swearing at the absent servants. 'Just wait until this is all over! If they think they can come and get their jobs back afterwards, they'll have to think again!'

He had an arthritic hip, which didn't help his temper. 'You must remember that your grandfather is old and often in pain,' Natasha's mother told her.

Prince Mikhail had gone to join the Tsar at the Front. Natasha felt anxious about her father. Her mother prayed a lot in front of the ikon of the Virgin Mary in her room.

'It is your father's duty to protect the Tsar, Natasha, and you should be proud of him,' her grandmother told her, adding, 'Though I would prefer that he was here protecting us!'

'We have Stepan and Pyotr,' said Natasha. The chief steward and the coachman were the only two male servants to have stayed. 'They are big and strong.'

'But they are not soldiers.'

Prince Ivan had been in the Cossacks himself when he was younger. He had laid out his sword in the hall, lest trouble come to their door. 'I am ready for them!' he would cry.

'He'd fall over the dashed thing if he tried to draw it!' said his wife in an aside, though Prince Ivan was hard of hearing anyway.

Natasha was still recovering from her accident and had been keeping to her room most of the time. Her mother kept telling her she should keep herself occupied and that sewing was a restful activity. Embroidery in particular was a very pleasant way to pass the time. Natasha, though she did persevere, did not find it particularly restful; she pricked her finger too often. But she did like wearing her jewelled thimble. And she loved the colours of the silken threads. She stopped frequently to admire both them and the thimble.

'It's pretty, isn't it, Lena?' She held the thimble up to the light and the tiny jewels sparkled.

'Very pretty.'

'I shall buy you a beautiful thimble for your next birthday.'

Lena merely smiled and carried on sewing. Her fingers moved swiftly and deftly over the soft velvet.

'You don't believe me?'

'People like me don't expect to have beautiful thimbles, Miss Natasha.'

'Well, you will! We'll go together to the Singer sewing shop on the Nevsky and I will buy you the most beautiful thimble in the whole shop.'

'Perhaps I would rather have a pretty ring? Or a bracelet?' Lena glanced over at the dresser on which lay a silver bracelet belonging to Natasha.

There was an abrupt knock on the door and it burst open to admit Pyotr. He stood there with snow on his hair and his cheeks red from the cold.

'The Tsar has abdicated!' he announced.

'Never!' cried Lena, jumping up and allowing the velvet dress to slide to the floor in a heap. But her eyes were gleaming.

'The Tsar has given up his *throne*?' stammered Natasha, unable to believe it.

'That's right, Miss Natasha. He had no choice in the end.' Pyotr shook his head. 'He was on his way back to St Petersburg. Revolutionaries stopped his train.'

'Revolutionaries?' repeated Natasha, still feeling stupified by the news.

'He'll be under armed guard now then?' said Lena and she looked at Natasha, reading her thoughts. Prince Mikhail would have been on the train.

'It's the end of an era,' said Pyotr, 'that's what they're saying.'

'It had to come,' said Lena.

Natasha pricked her finger again, but this time the needle went deeper and blood spurted on to her embroidery and ruined it.

SEVEN

WAR AND PEACE

Alex and Duncan went straight away to the library to look for *War and Peace*. The room was walled with books on three sides from floor to ceiling. On the remaining wall, on either side of the window, hung paintings, the most prominent of which was one of St Petersburg in winter. The city skyscape was broken by numerous golden spires and domes, which glittered against the bright blue of the sky. Winter was magical, Natasha used to say, with the snow lying deep and crisp and even. She had loved skating on the frozen river and going for sleigh rides into the countryside. It was magical as long as one had a fur rug to cover one and a warm, dry house to go back to.

On the table under the window stood a photograph of Nikolai, the last Tsar of the Russian Empire, with his wife and children on the veranda of their summer palace. The four young grand-duchesses, Olga, Tatiana, Marie and Anastasia, wore long white, sashed dresses and broad, ribboned hats, and Alexei, the son of the Tsar, heir to a throne he would never inherit, a sailor suit. Natasha had known the children. She had always spoken of them sadly for they had all been murdered by the Communists.

The books in the library were roughly classified, but only roughly. Biographies and travel books could be found amongst novels and volumes of poetry. Anna had said she must set herself to putting them in order one day. But there had never seemed to be time. And now the books that had belonged to Natasha would be taken away by Boris. Unless they found the will.

Alex trawled along the shelves, letting his eyes slide over the titles. He had to stand on the library steps to reach the upper shelves. 'Tolstoy!' he read at length. '*Anna Karenina*.' He touched the spine and his fingers came away dusty.

'You could be close,' said Duncan from below.

But Alex still could not see *War and Peace*.

The front doorbell broke the silence and then they heard the postie shouting from the hall, 'Post!' He always came straight in. The front door wasn't locked, except when they went to bed.

'In here,' called Alex.

There were a couple of bills in the mail and a letter with a London postmark.

'How's the lassie doing?' asked the postman.

'Not much change, I'm afraid,' said Duncan.

'Aye, it's a bad business. Remember me to Anna when you're speaking to her.'

'We will,' promised Duncan.

The postie left and Duncan opened the London letter. It was from Cousin Boris.

'Maybe he's changed his mind,' said Alex.

'Not a chance, son!'

'What does he say, Dad?'

44

'How sorry he is about Sonya, et cetera. But repeating, of course, that he could not be held in any way to blame.'

'Except that if he hadn't come Sonya wouldn't be lying in hospital now at –' Alex had been going to say, 'at death's door,' but had bitten it back. What if Sonya did die? He hadn't allowed himself to think that, until now. 'Dad, she will get better, won't she?'

'She's got to!' said Duncan. 'And we've got to find this annoying will so that we have a home for her to come back to when she's better. Do you know, Alex, there's no way Natasha could have climbed up those steps.'

'That's true.' Alex jumped down, half stumbling as he landed. He ended up sitting on the floor. He glanced at the shelf level with his eyes and saw *War and Peace*! How could he have missed it? He had already looked there. He eased the book carefully out of its slot. It wasn't as dusty as some of the others. Someone must have taken it out of the shelf not too long ago.

He squatted beside his father's chair and opened the book at the first page. The paper was thin and yellowed at the edges.

'What is it going to tell us, I wonder,' said Duncan.

The first chapter was called 'Anna Scherer's Soirée' and was set in St Petersburg in July 1805. They stared at it.

'Well now, that doesn't seem to be much help,' said Duncan.

'It's an awfully long book,' said Alex, turning to the back page. 'One thousand three hundred and fifty two pages! We can't read through all that.'

45

'No, I don't think we can.'

Alex flicked through some of the pages, but there were no markings on any of them. Then he held the book by its covers to see if he could shake anything loose.

'Careful now,' cautioned his father. 'It's an old book. Don't break the spine.'

Cautiously, Alex swung the book from side to side. And out fluttered a slip of thin white paper. He gasped and his father drew in his breath sharply. Neither spoke for a moment. Could it be the will?

Alex's hands trembled as he lifted the paper from the floor. He recognized Natasha's handwriting with its strong loops and curls. He swallowed, before reading the message aloud.

'"*Congratulations! You've reached the first post in the hunt for the will. You were always good at treasure hunts, so I knew you'd find me.*

'"*So, for my next clue, see if you can find me again.*"'

Alex looked up.

'Is that all?' asked his father.

'That's all.'

EIGHT

SONYA SLEEPS ON

'It's Mum here, Sonya,' said Anna, for what must have been the hundredth time. 'I'm sitting right beside you and I'm holding your hand. It's a lovely day outside, fresh and bright. I can see blue sky through the window with a few puffy white clouds. The sun is coming into the room lightening it up.'

Anna's own life had been reduced to this small room, except for brief walks in the city streets. At night she slept on a truckle bed, often lying awake, listening to the sound of Sonya's breathing. What had Sonya's life been reduced to? Was there anything going on inside her head? There must be! She wasn't brain dead. The x-rays and scans had seemed to indicate that she was not. At times, a range of emotions appeared to cross her face. She would smile almost, then frown, then show signs of anxiety and Anna would have to bend over her and say, 'It's all right, Sonya, it's all right. You're safe and I am here with you.'

'Dad sends his love,' she said now. 'So does Alex. Alex says to tell you that Tobias is missing you and you are to come back soon and have a long ride round the loch shore.' Anna talked on, mentioning names of family and friends. She spoke too, of Natasha. Duncan had said, 'Talk to her about Natasha. She was so much a part of her life and her imagination.'

NINE

'*I* have an errand to do, Natasha,' said her mother. 'I would like you to come with me.'

Natasha was surprised that her mother would want to go out, considering the dangers that lurked in the streets, but she ran at once to fetch her cloak. Her mother seldom wanted to do anything these days; she seemed poorly much of the time and often stayed in bed all day.

'It is her spirit that is low,' said Lena. 'She is pining for your father, poor woman.'

Prince Mikhail had managed to escape when the Tsar's train was stopped by the revolutionaries and he was now in southern Russia with the White Army, fighting the Red Army. There was no battle left to be fought in St Petersburg. The Bolsheviks were completely in control of the city, conducting a reign of terror. They took people away in the night who were never seen again. In the provinces, the Whites, who represented the old order, were losing ground. At least, so said the newspapers, which were censored according to Natasha's grandfather, who refused to believe any of it.

49

'They are full of lies, the Bolsheviks! They tell the papers what to print. My regiment and my son's regiment would never be defeated. Can you imagine, the Cossacks on their knees!'

Natasha prayed that her father would not be on his knees as she went up to her room.

'You can't wear that,' objected Lena, when she saw her dressed in her cloak. 'Not with all that fur trimming! Put on a dark-coloured coat that won't attract attention. And wear a kerchief to cover your hair. If you don't, you will look like a little princess. And princesses are not in favour any more!' Everyone in the house looked now to Lena for advice, even Prince Ivan, although he would not have admitted it.

Natasha's mother was ready, dressed also in a dark coat with a kerchief covering her hair.

'Have you got the piece of paper?' Lena asked her.

Princess Eva nodded.

They left the house by the back door after Stepan had checked the street.

'Where are we going, Mama?' asked Natasha.

'You'll see soon enough.'

It was a relief to be outside and to smell the fresh air. They headed away from the river towards the main thoroughfare. Although the sun was shining brightly on the golden domes of the city, the wind blowing up the wide Nevsky Boulevard carried a chilly sting in its tail. Natasha tucked her hand into the crook of her mother's arm and drew close to her.

The boulevard used to bustle with carriages and horse buses and motor cars, while pedestrians thronged the pavements on their way to the shops and cafes.

Today, the street was almost deserted. The eerie quiet made Natasha want to keep looking over her shoulder. They passed a group of beggars. Two of the women clutched babies to their chest. As Natasha and her mother drew level they held out cupped hands. 'For the love of God, Madame! For the children's sake!'

'Can't you give them something, Mama?' pleaded Natasha.

'No, I can't.' Her mother walked on with her head down. 'I have nothing to give.'

Natasha glanced back. The women were still holding out their hands forlornly. Quickly she unwound the cashmere scarf from around her neck and tossed it to them. They scrambled to reach it, each seizing an end. Their voices rose up in dispute.

'Now look what you've done!' said Natasha's mother. 'What are they going to do with it? Cut it in two?'

'Perhaps,' said Natasha defiantly. 'It might make a scarf for each baby.'

'And what about you? Your neck will get cold and then you'll start coughing.'

Natasha pulled up the collar of her coat. 'I have plenty of scarves at home.'

'Not so many as before.'

That was true. Some of her clothes were now being worn by young relatives of Lena. 'You don't need so many pairs of stockings, do you, Miss Natasha?' she'd say. 'I have a niece the same size as you. She has no stockings. Her legs are bare. You wouldn't want her to go cold in winter, would you?' Of course Natasha would not.

'Please don't give anything else away!' said Princess

Eva. 'Lena is sucking us dry enough without you helping.'

'Lena helps us too!'

'She looks after her own interests. Everyone does these days.'

These days. It was a phrase constantly on Natasha's mother's lips and on those of the grandparents. Everything is different these days . . .

They passed other beggars. Some stood simply with a hand stretched out, as if the effort to move would be too much for them. Others, the ill and the crippled, sat in doorways, crying out in thin voices to passers-by. For the love of God . . .

'Don't look at them,' said Princess Eva. 'It is best not to engage their eyes since there is nothing we can do.'

They stopped to read a notice fastened to a drain-pipe. 'For Sale,' it said. 'A fine mahogany sideboard, English, Sheraton. Also, a grand piano, Bechstein, and two fur coats, tailored in Berlin.' An address on the fashionable Fontanka Canal was given at the bottom. The writing had blurred with the rain and was barely readable. Another family had fallen on hard times. Princess Eva sighed.

On the next corner, a woman stood like a statue, holding out her arms, over which lay a long hank of hair.

'Is she selling her *hair*?' asked Natasha.

'Everything is for sale these days,' said her mother.

Not a muscle in the woman's face moved as they went by.

'Now let me see,' said Princess Eva, consulting the piece of paper that she had been given by Lena. 'Yes, we turn down here.'

They entered a side street.

'It should be just a few doors along.'

Many of the shops were closed, having nothing to sell. The one Princess Eva was looking for had a curtain drawn across its window though a dim light could be seen within. The door jangled as they opened it.

The owner, an elderly man with a spade-shaped beard, was sitting behind the counter wrapped in a bulky beaver coat. The temperature stood no higher than zero, but few people in the city had any form of heating. In the Denisov palace they had a few skimpy fires, which were kept going with old pieces of wood collected by Pyotr in the streets.

'Yes?' The man did not get up.

'I believe you buy jewellery?' Princess Eva spoke nervously. She had never been involved in such dealings before.

'What is it you wish to sell?'

She took a velvet bag from her pocket and with trembling fingers withdrew two necklaces. They sparkled in the poor light. The man scooped them up into his gnarled hands. His eyes glistened, like the rubies and emeralds in front of him. He named a price.

'Is that all?' cried Princess Eva. 'But these are valuable necklaces. They are heirlooms belonging to my family. The stones are genuine.'

'I can offer no more. Jewellery is not easy to sell these days. Who can buy?'

Lena had told them that there were people around who could buy jewellery and other expensive items. They were people who had not had money formerly, but now that they were in power they seemed to have found riches to go with it.

'I am sorry, Madame, but that is my only offer.'

'Don't do it, Mama!' cried Natasha. 'We'll find a way. We'll sell something else.'

'I have no choice,' said her mother, and then to the man, 'I will take it.'

He gave them the money and they left the shop.

'I have things I could have sold,' said Natasha.

'Such as?'

'My sewing basket. It has little pearls on it. My amber trinket box, that Papa brought back from Latvia. My music box, the one that came from Paris. My thimble.' Here, Natasha's voice faltered.

'You are never to let that go! If you do bad luck, even worse than we have at present, will follow you for the rest of your life. It was given to you as a lucky charm at birth by your godmother.'

'The other things then?' said Natasha. She wouldn't *want* to part with any of them, they were dear to her, but if her mother could give up her necklaces she should be able to make sacrifices too.

'Nobody would give more than a sou for any of them!'

Natasha suspected that her mother was right. When people were suffering so much who would want to play with a musical box? She felt guilty when she did.

The light was failing rapidly and small flakes of snow were beginning to drift down from the darkening sky. They feared the long winter ahead, with so little fuel available. They had already shut up several of the rooms in the palace.

Natasha and her mother walked back down the boulevard and cut through to the river. When they reached the English embankment they saw three men in uniform coming towards them. They wore five-pointed red stars on their helmets and red rosettes on their coats and they carried their rifles slung casually over their shoulders.

'The Red Guard,' said Princess Eva in a low voice. 'Look away from them.'

Natasha did as commanded. The pavement was broad and there would have been plenty of room for them to pass, had the guards allowed it. Instead, they swerved into their path and forced them to stop. The men's eyes narrowed. Would they realize that they were from an aristocratic family? Lena said you could always pick out people like them, no matter what they dressed in. It was just a look they had.

'One of *them*!' said the guard in the middle and he spat straight into the face of Princess Eva. She winced and brought her arm up to cover her face. Natasha cried out.

'You can't do that to my mother!'

'Can't I, indeed, young miss?' The guard seized Natasha's arm in a grip that made her bite her lip so that she wouldn't cry out again. 'I will do whatever I want to do!'

'Leave her, please,' begged her mother. 'She's only a child.'

The soldier pushed Natasha roughly away so that she staggered and went down on one knee with a sharp crack. 'Be careful how you speak to us in future!'

The men moved on, laughing. Natasha picked herself up and took her mother's hand.

'We can't help it that we were born in a palace, can we?' she said.

They walked quickly on, breaking into a run as they neared their door. It was opened immediately by Stepan. There seemed to be a lot of noise going on in the house.

'What's happening?' asked Princess Eva.

'We have lodgers,' said Stepan.

'Lodgers?'

Stepan closed and barred the door behind them. Princess Olga appeared from the salon waving her hands about. They were less plump than they used to be. She, like everyone else, had lost weight.

'Eva, this is dreadful! The place has been taken over by a rabble! There are some upstairs, some downstairs.'

'Where is Lena?'

'I am here!' Lena emerged from the kitchen with a train of people behind her, a man and a woman carrying bundles, followed by three, four, five, six children, of varying heights and sizes.

'Who are these people?' demanded Princess Eva.

'They have been living in two rooms, two miserable rooms with a leaking roof and water running down the walls. Can you imagine, Madame, what that would be like? The children have terrible coughs.'

As if to illustrate, several of them began to cough. They had hacking barks which, once started, appeared difficult to control. Princess Olga had placed her hands over her ears and was moaning.

'We shall never have peace again! Never!'

'How did they get here, Lena?' asked Princess Eva. 'Did they just come in off the street?'

'The Red Guard brought them.'

That silenced the princess.

'I am putting them in the Rose suite,' said Lena.

'The Rose suite?' said Princess Olga. 'Those are our best guest bedrooms. Ambassadors have slept there.'

'We won't be having guests any more,' said her daughter-in-law flatly.

Lena began to climb the stairs. The family of eight went after her, casting awed looks at the large gilt-framed paintings on the walls. Natasha and her mother and grandmother watched them go.

They were to find that the other guest bedrooms had already been filled, as had been the music room and Princess Olga's private salon. In all, four families had been moved into the house. Lena would now sleep in what had formerly been the nursery, which adjoined Natasha's room. It was more comfortable than the old servants' quarters, she said. Her bedroom had been poky and dark.

Lena ran the household, keeping order, quelling arguments and potential fights when they erupted between the tenant families, who vied with one another over fuel and food supplies and the use of the kitchen stove. The kitchen seethed from early morning until midnight. The only room, apart from their bedrooms, that the Denisovs retained for themselves was the salon.

'Lock the door of your bedroom when you leave it,' Lena advised Natasha. 'They are desperate, some of them. They will steal anything you have and I cannot have eyes everywhere.'

'God knows,' said Prince Ivan, 'before this is done we shall all be murdered in our beds!'

TEN

LOOKING FOR NATASHA

'*See if you can find me again*,' Natasha had written.

They were puzzling over the clue when they heard a car pull up outside. Alex went to the window to look. The car wasn't local.

'They might be looking for B&B.'

'We should have taken the sign down,' said Duncan.

Since Sonya's accident they had not been able to have boarders. It wasn't possible without Anna. Already they had turned away two couples and two families.

'I know, I've been meaning to do it. I'd better go and see them.'

Two men were getting out of the car when Alex opened the front door. One of them, the passenger, was carrying a large camera. It looked like the kind of camera that would be used for commercial purposes. Alex frowned.

'Hello there!' the driver called out heartily. 'You the son of the house? Are your parents about?'

'My father.'

'Could we see him?'

'Who shall I say?'

'Mr Trotter. From Trotter, Smythe and Pendle-bury.'

'Lawyers?'

'Estate agents.'

'Oh.' Alex's heart dropped.

'I'm acting for Mr Malenkov,' said Mr Trotter. 'I've come to make an evaluation of the property.'

Alex looked at the photographer.

'This is Ronnie,' said Mr Trotter. 'He's going to take a few photographs. For the brochure. For when the house goes up for sale. Mr Malenkov thought it would save time if he just came with me now.'

So Cousin Boris was taking it for granted that his way was clear to inherit Natasha's estate! Alex thought of the latest clue: '*See if you can find me again.*' The 'me' hadn't been underlined on the piece of paper, but it was in Alex's head.

Mr Trotter had turned to survey the landscape. 'Nice site. Secluded. Peaceful. Away from it all. Good views over the Atlantic. Facing south and west. Excellent.' He swivelled back to regard the house. 'Place could do with a bit of a face-lift, but basically it looks like a good property. Haven't seen any sign of dry rot, have you, lad?'

'Dry rot?' Alex was startled, for he was still thinking of Natasha. 'No.' Not that he would know it if he saw it. Or wet rot either.

'Been living here long, have you?'

'Eight years. Mr Malenkov is going to put us out if he inherits.'

'Look, son, this is none of my business. That's between you and Mr Malenkov, right? I can't afford to let myself get mixed up in family feuds or things of that nature. I've got a job to do. I've been engaged to come here and survey the property.'

After he'd had a few words with Duncan, the estate agent got to work on the house and outbuildings and then the land. He measured and recorded, measured and recorded, and the photographer followed on behind, clicking his camera.

'That's all he sees the place as – a property,' said Alex. He and his father were in the kitchen eating bread and lentil soup for their lunch. His father had made the soup. 'He doesn't seem to realize it's our home.'

'You can't blame him,' said Duncan. 'It's his job.'

The door opened and the man himself put his head round. 'Ah, there you are.' He sniffed. 'Something smells good. Couldn't make us a cup of tea, could you, lad? Thirsty work this.'

Alex got up unwillingly and filled the kettle. His mother always offered tea or coffee to anyone coming to work in the house.

'Could we offer you some soup?' said Duncan.

'Wouldn't say no,' said Mr Trotter. 'Not much in the way of restaurants around these parts. Couldn't cope myself with living so far from everything. Enough soup for two, have you?'

'There should be.' Duncan rolled himself over to the cooker and turned on the heat under the soup pot.

Mr Trotter went back out into the hall and called, 'Ronnie, are you there? Fancy a bowl of soup to warm the cockles of your heart?'

'Not much chance of that,' muttered Alex.

'Now we have to be hospitable, Alex,' said his father. 'Your mother would want us to be.'

The men came in and seated themselves at the table. Alex served them.

'This is really good of you,' said Ronnie.

'Much appreciated,' added Mr Trotter.

'Rough business,' said Ronnie, 'getting turfed out of your home.'

'Perhaps I can help you find another house, Mr McKinnon,' said Mr Trotter. 'I have one or two items on my books that might interest you. I could send you particulars.'

'We're not in the market, I'm afraid. We don't have any capital.'

'That's what comes of living in someone else's house.' Mr Trotter shook his head. 'It's usually a mistake. You've no security.'

'We liked living with Natasha,' said Alex. 'She was like a grandmother to us and the house was too big for her to manage on her own.' He went on to tell the men about the will.

'It might not even exist,' warned Mr Trotter. He knew of cases where people had said they had made a will when they hadn't. 'They say it just to keep in with you while they're alive.'

'Natasha wasn't like that,' said Alex indignantly.

'You never know though, do you, what folk are really thinking inside their heads?'

When the men were ready to leave, Alex accompanied them to their car.

'You keep looking for that will!' said Ronnie, as he stowed his cameras in the boot.

'And do the lottery!' added Mr Trotter.

They had tried that.

Alex waved them off. They hadn't been so bad.

After all, Mr Trotter wasn't the one who would evict them. As Alex went back inside he heard the phone ringing. He lifted the receiver in the hall.

'Hello, is that you, Alex?' It was his mother. 'How are things there?'

'Fine,' he said. He wasn't going to tell her about the estate agents. That would only give her something else to worry about.

'How's Sonya?' He hated asking, in case the news was bad.

'Very restless at the moment. It's as if something is troubling her deep down, wherever she is.'

After he'd rung off, Alex found his father in the library frowning over Natasha's latest clue. He looked up and asked first about Sonya and was given the usual answer.

'Pity she's not here to help us. She could read Natasha's mind better than any of us. I've been trying to think of any other book with a character called Natasha in it. My mind's a complete blank.'

'Wasn't Natasha a princess? Her father was a prince, at any rate.'

'Yes, she would have been. There must be loads of children's stories about princesses. *The Princess and the Pea.*'

'*Sleeping Beauty.*' That made Alex think about Sonya and he felt a pang. 'She became a princess when the prince married her. Maybe I should have a look in a book of fairy tales?'

He found a number of stories featuring princesses but no slips of paper. His father was still frowning.

'Isn't there a novel about a little princess or something of that sort? It probably wasn't your kind of book!'

'It might have been when I was very small.' Alex grinned. His mother and Natasha had read stories about everything under the sun to them. He was racking his brains. 'I seem to remember something about a girl who was rich and then became poor when her father lost everything. Can't remember who wrote it though.'

He surveyed the shelves. Then he saw it: *A Little Princess* by Frances Hodgson Burnett. He lifted it out.

It was an old copy and it had belonged to his mother. Her name was written on the fly leaf and the date, 1964. She must have been about nine years old then.

Alex remembered the story now. The girl in the novel hadn't been a real princess, but because she was wealthy she had seemed like one, whereas Natasha had been a proper princess who had lost her status when she was a child. She had always said that was of no importance to her. To have survived and had the chance to make a new life had been the most important thing.

Tucked into the middle of the book was a sheet of thin white paper. Alex drew it out. He read the clue to his father.

'"*Take the hint. There's treachery waiting in the wings.*"'

ELEVEN

*E*arly one morning, another group of refugees arrived looking for shelter. Stepan, on opening the door to a knock, found them standing on the step, clutching their bundles like any other homeless family. Count Leo Malenkov, brother of Princess Eva, his wife, Marie, and their small son, Kyril, looked cold and bedraggled. There was no sign of a carriage outside. Stepan concluded that they must have walked from their house half a mile away.

'Is my sister at home?' asked Count Leo.

Stepan helped them to come inside with their luggage. They had brought little, considering what they must have owned at one time. He showed them into the salon and went to call Princess Eva.

'They've come to call at this hour? My brother? What can he want?'

'I fear he has been evicted, Madame.'

Princess Eva rapped on her daughter's door. 'Dress quickly. Your Uncle Leo and Aunt Marie are here with your cousin Kyril. Perhaps you can amuse the child.'

Natasha was not fond of amusing that particular

child, who cried at the slightest provocation, but she did as she was told and, a few minutes later, followed her mother downstairs. Kyril was whining as she opened the door.

'Ah, here is your cousin Natasha!' cried his mother with relief, propelling him in her direction.

Natasha gathered him on to her knee. Her mother said that Marie had no knack with children, or with anything else. Eva was not overly fond of her sister-in-law. If they were going to have to live under the same roof it would not be easy. But then, nothing that was happening was easy. And regardless of differences, the families would stick together. They believed blood to be thicker than water.

'So, Leo,' said Eva with a sigh, 'you've been evicted?'

'I'm afraid so.'

'Yet I thought you favoured a revolution?' Leo was a qualified medical doctor and had worked with the poor. But that had obviously not protected him. The fact that he was a count had outweighed his good works. Eva's father-in-law used to call him a Red lackey. They had not got on.

'Change had to come,' said Leo. 'There was so much corruption and injustice. But not this kind of change. Not this bloodbath.' He shook his head wearily. 'I fear it will bring its own forms of corruption. It already has.'

'I suppose we're lucky that we've been allowed to keep a few rooms for ourselves!' said Eva.

Stepan went off to the kitchen to see if he could find something for the new arrivals to eat. Lena kept stores locked up in a special cupboard for the family.

Anything left in the open was immediately snatched up by whoever came along first. There was so sign of Lena or the key for the cupboard. Stepan managed to find some slices of stale bread and a half-empty pot of thin jam.

He apologized when he brought them back to the salon.

'It's not your fault, Stepan,' said Eva. 'You don't have to apologize. Do you think you could light the fire? It's freezing in here.'

'I'll see if I can find wood, Madame.'

'And find Lena too! She will know what to do. Where is she anyway?'

Natasha said nothing. She knew that Lena did not like to rise too early. She said she had had to rise early all her life. 'I do not intend to do it now. I have known enough cold dark mornings.'

Lena appeared half an hour later, followed by Stepan carrying a few sticks. Natasha looked up, startled, as Lena came in, and saw that her mother was reacting in a similar way. Lena was wearing a blue chenille dress with an embroidered collar. It belonged to Princess Eva. Or rather, it had belonged to her. Neither of them said anything. They were gradually learning.

'Where are my brother and his family to sleep, Lena?' asked Princess Eva.

'There are no rooms left, as you know, except for this one. Everything else is taken.'

'But this is the salon!'

'I'm afraid they will have to sleep here. Or else it is the kitchen.' Lena shrugged.

'The kitchen! But that is full of –' Princess Eva

broke off. She had been going to say, 'tramps and thieves,' but had thought better of it. Leo himself had warned her to curb her tongue, especially when speaking to servants. You never knew whose side they might be on. Some of them were reputed to be spying for the Bolsheviks. Eva had also warned her daughter to be careful what she said to Lena. Natasha had retorted with annoyance, 'But she's my friend, Mama!'

'We can sleep here,' said Leo. 'We shall be pleased enough with this.'

When Princess Olga came down to partake of her morning tea she was far from pleased.

'But this is the only salon left! Where are we to sit?'

'Leo and Marie will take up only a small amount of room,' said Eva.

Princess Olga regarded the child Kyril. 'I like peace and quiet in my salon. The rest of the house is in a state of chaos.'

Leo began to apologize for causing such inconvenience, but his sister cut him off.

'They have nowhere else to go,' she informed her mother-in-law. 'I cannot let my brother and his family freeze to death on the streets. You would not expect me to, would you? If Mikhail were here he would not allow them to.'

'Of course I don't want them to freeze to death,' said Princess Olga tetchily. 'How I wish poor dear Mikhail was here.'

Prince Ivan entered. 'This is absolutely preposterous!' Colour had mounted high on his cheekbones so that the skin had taken on a purple tinge. His wife put a restraining hand on his arm, but he paid no attention. She feared he might get so wound up one day that he would have a heart attack. 'How dare they put you out of your own home, Leo! Turn you into the streets like common riff-raff! And after what you did for them. Those bloody Bolsheviks! Thank God my son is still out there fighting them! The White Army will be victorious in the end, you'll see. Our time will come again!'

'Hush, Father-in-law,' said Eva, glancing at the doorway. Lena was hovering in the hall with a feather duster in her hand, which she was making no attempt to use.

'I don't wish to hush! We have done too much hushing.'

'Come and have some tea,' said Eva, going to the samovar. They still had a little tea left, which they mixed with dried herbs.

'Tastes of dried hay,' he declared after a sip.

There came a loud knock on the outside door. Every time it happened they froze and stopped whatever they had been doing. They kept their eyes down. They heard Stepan go to the door and then voices split the silence, raised, demanding voices. Even the small child in the room was still, as if he could scent the fear of his elders.

The salon door was opened. Stepan tried to speak, but was pushed roughly aside. Four Red Guard entered, wearing their hats and rifles.

'Which of you is Prince Ivan Denisov?'

The prince straightened himself up.

'Come with us, Denisov! Straight away! And be quick about it!'

'You can't do this!' The prince started to bluster and to back away.

He was seized by two of the guards, each of whom took an arm.

'You can't take him away!' cried Princess Olga. 'He's an old man.'

'And not well,' said Leo quietly, stepping forward. 'I would ask you to show mercy on him.'

'He's an enemy of the people,' said one of the guards. 'Enemies deserve no mercy.'

'He hasn't even got his coat on,' cried his wife. 'He'll catch his death.'

'He won't need a coat for long!' joked the guard and the other three laughed.

Princess Olga advanced towards them with her hands outstretched. 'At least let me –'

'You can say goodbye.'

She said it in a whisper. Prince Ivan made an attempt to say something in return, but was unable to produce a sound.

'Right, let's get moving!' He was prodded in the back with a rifle butt. He stumbled forward.

The guards departed with their prisoner. Those left behind listened to the sound of their feet dying away on the pavement outside. When they had gone, Princess Olga began to weep, very quietly. Her daughter-in-law put her arms around her. Tears flooded Natasha's own eyes and spilled down her cheeks. Leo shut the door, closing the family off from the rest of the world.

TWELVE

TREACHERY IN THE WINGS

'*C*an you read out the clue again, Alex?' asked his father.

'"*Take the hint. There's treachery waiting in the wings.*"'

'Sounds like Shakespeare. Try *Julius Caesar.*'

Shakespeare's plays were all on the same shelf. There were no pieces of paper in *Julius Caesar.*

'I'll just try the lot, shall I, Dad? I expect there's quite a bit of treachery in a number of them!'

Alex went through the shelf of plays and found nothing.

'Maybe I should take out every book on the shelves and shake them,' he suggested.

'Then we might end up with the clues all jumbled together. And not all the papers drop out easily, as you know. You'd have to go through each book page by page. It would take hours. There are thousands of books on those shelves. Let's go back to thinking about treachery. Does it suggest anything to you?'

'There's treachery in *Treasure Island.*'

Alex found *Treasure Island* easily for this was a book he had read himself and so he recognized the spine.

He took it down and carefully swung it to and fro. Nothing fell out.

'There aren't so many pages in it,' said Duncan. 'Let's just look through the lot.'

They went carefully through the book, page by page, to no avail.

'Waiting in the wings does make it sound like something to do with the theatre,' reflected Duncan.

'What about take the hint? Do you think Natasha just meant "hint" to be another word for "clue"?'

'Who knows? But let's think about "hint". What other words can you think of for it?'

'Tip?'

'Suggestion? A hint is a mild sort of suggestion. Also, you can talk about a hint of colour.' Duncan pursed his lips. 'I don't feel we're getting anywhere, do you?'

'Betrayal,' said Alex, throwing in the word for consideration. 'Treason.'

'Perfidy,' said Duncan. 'Deceit. Disloyalty.'

They kept turning the same words over and over again, hoping for a flash of enlightenment.

'Treason sounds good,' said Duncan. 'What about a hint of treason? Something like that.'

And then, suddenly, Alex got it and he couldn't understand why he hadn't thought of it before.

'A hint could be a cue for an actor in the theatre, couldn't it?'

'It could,' acknowledged his father.

'What about *Cue for Treason*? It's a novel by Geoffrey Trease.'

THIRTEEN

ST PETERSBURG, APRIL 1918
NEWS FROM THE FRONT

*T*hey had realized for some time that they would have to try to find a way to leave St Petersburg. It would not be easy; far from it. That was why they had delayed their departure. Princess Olga was another reason. Following her husband's arrest and execution, she was so ill and distraught that it was impossible to consider taking her with them. She would never have survived the journey. Then, in February, she fell, broke her hip and subsequently contracted pneumonia and died. Leo had done what he could, but he had lacked the drugs to help her.

In February, the snow still lay deep, with temperatures dropping regularly to well below freezing. Inside the house, icicles hung from the window ledges. They huddled round makeshift fires, with a broken-up kitchen dresser, a couple of chairs, even table legs, as well as whatever Stepan could scavenge outside, providing the fuel. Outside, the street sweepers heaped up piles of snow with their flat wooden shovels and lit bonfires in an attempt to melt it. The river was frozen solid. There was little change through March.

In mid-April, they heard the first cracking of the ice

on the river, heralding the beginning of a thaw. The days remained cold, however, and Leo said they must wait until it was a little warmer. And then the soldier came with the news that was to push them into action.

He arrived dressed in ragged civilian clothes, his boots riddled with holes and held on to his skinny, infected ankles with pieces of string. Stepan left him standing on the doorstep while he went to call Princess Eva. Natasha was with her in her room.

'He says he's from your husband's regiment, Madame.'

They knew immediately that the news would be bad. They hurried downstairs. The man on the cold step looked barely able to stand.

'Come inside, please,' said Princess Eva. She closed the door behind him. They stood in the porch. 'You seem very weak?'

'I am, Madame. I've walked most of the way from Omsk.'

'*Walked?* That is a very long way. What news do you bring?'

'Bad news, I'm afraid, Madame.' He lifted his rheumy eyes to look at her.

'Oh no!' she cried.

'I'm sorry,' he said.

Natasha seized her mother's hand and held on to it tightly. She had long thought that there was not much hope of seeing her father again. In his sparkling blue Cossack uniform, he seemed like someone who had belonged to a different life.

'When your husband was dying on the field he asked me to come and tell you, Madame, in person.

I was with him at the end, you see.'

'Did he —?' The princess faltered. 'Did he die quickly? Did he suffer much?'

'He went in minutes. I stayed with him.'

'How kind you are. What is your name?'

'Rufus.'

'Where will you go after this, Rufus?'

'Home to my village, in the north.'

'Will you walk? But how can you, in the state that you're in?'

He shrugged.

'If you will wait here, Rufus, I will find you some clothes and food.' Princess Eva did not dare ask him to come further than the porch. It was said that the Secret Police had a spy inside every house. Leo had warned them to be careful what they said in front of anyone outside the family. Every time they heard a loud knock on the door, they feared that the Red Guard might have come for him. They thought Leo had been spared only because he was a doctor and there was a scarcity of medical people in the city. Many had fled or been taken away. He was still working long hours amongst the city's poor.

'Thank you, Madame.' Rufus tried to touch his forelock, but his arm was too weak.

'Don't.' The princess put her hand on his arm. She no longer expected such gestures from people.

'Who is there?' asked a voice behind them.

They turned to see Lena.

'He is a poor beggar, that is all,' said Princess Eva. 'I want to give him some clothes and a little food.'

'We have neither to spare.'

'Natasha, go up to my room,' said her mother, 'and

bring down some clothes of your father's. Some warm clothes. And boots. Here is the key.'

Natasha took the key and fled up the stairs. *My father is dead. My father is dead.* As she went, the words pounded inside her head like the heavy beat of a drum. She unlocked the door of her mother's room with fumbling hands. They had hidden some of her father's clothes underneath the bed. The rest had been dispersed amongst the lodgers by Lena. Natasha dragged out the bundle of clothes. Her father would never wear any of these things again. Never! She caught her breath. A pain had flashed through her heart like a streak of lightning.

The door behind her opened and Lena poked her blue-kerchiefed head round.

'Can I help you, Natasha?'

'No, thank you, I can manage.'

Natasha swiftly extracted from the bundle a pair of heavy tweed trousers, a woollen overshirt, some socks, a fur hat, a shuba and a pair of brown leather knee-length boots.

'I didn't know your mother had all those clothes there.' Lena came over to the bed. 'Why is she giving all this to a tramp who calls at the door?'

'I don't know.' Natasha did not look up.

'I hardly think she could have taken a fancy to him?' Lena gave an unpleasant laugh. 'Have you ever seen him before?'

'No, never.'

Natasha stood up, clothes spilling from her arms.

'It's crazy to give so much to a stranger who just knocks at the door,' said Lena.

She reached out to take something. Natasha backed

away, trying desperately to hold on to the garments. One of the boots slipped from her grasp and toppled to the floor. In a flash, Lena had picked it up.

'This is very fine leather,' she said, stroking it. 'So supple! It is not often one comes across leather like this. Your father liked to wear top quality clothes, did he not? They're much too good for a tramp.'

'But the poor man's boots are falling to bits!'

'My brother would like a pair of boots like these. Give me the other one, please, Natasha!'

'No.'

'I insist!'

'What's going on?' Princess Eva had come to see why they were taking so long.

'I want to give these boots to my brother, Madame,' said Lena. 'And the shuba. He is in need of a warm overcoat.'

'So is the man at the door.'

'You seem very concerned about this man?' Lena's eyes narrowed. They looked like a cat's eyes, thought Natasha. The eyes of a cat confronting its prey.

'These clothes belonged to my husband. I shall give them to whoever I wish.' The princess was doing her best to control her voice. 'It is not your place, Lena, to challenge whom I give them to.'

'So, what is my place?' asked Lena softly. She gave a little smile though her eyes remained cold.

Princess Eva made no reply.

'The clothes *belonged* to your husband, did you say?' continued Lena.

'Belong still, I hope,' replied the princess, realizing her mistake. She did not want Lena to guess that the man in the porch had brought news of Prince

76

Mikhail's death. If she did, then she might suspect that he was a soldier who had fought with the White Army and she might denounce him to the Red Guard. 'So give me the boot, please!' Eva held out her hand.

Lena stared defiantly back, making no move to pass the boot over. For a moment it seemed that there would be no resolution. Natasha glanced at each of their faces in turn. Both looked determined not to give way. Eva reached out and tugged the boot sharply from Lena's hands.

'Give me the other one, please, Tasha dear,' said her mother. 'And the overcoat. Can you carry the rest? I will lock the door.' She stood on the threshold waiting. Lena hesitated for a moment then, with a toss of the head, she left the room.

Natasha had never known her mother act so forcefully. But she knew what the cost would be: they had made an enemy of Lena.

FOURTEEN

CUE FOR TREASON

Alex spent nearly an hour looking for Geoffrey Trease's book. He felt convinced that it would be the answer to the clue. His eyes were beginning to blur with the effort of reading titles, some of them so faded they were almost illegible. Yet he had the feeling he ought to be able to recognize the book straight away, for it was one that, again, he had read himself. Also, it was newish, at least compared with a lot of the dusty tomes, and so the title should still stand out. He frowned.

'You wouldn't have had it up in your room?' suggested Duncan.

Alex didn't think so – it was a while since he had read it – but he went and looked anyway. When you were embarked on a search you couldn't afford to ignore anything. He came back down to the library empty-handed. And then he remembered!

'I lent it to Iain two or three months ago. I don't think he ever gave it back.' Iain was one of his school friends. 'I hope he hasn't lost the clue.' It was an appalling thought that their hunt could end right there. It would have been only too easy for Iain to have come across the piece of paper and, thinking it was of no importance, thrown it away.

'Go and ring him,' said Duncan.

Iain's mother answered the phone. Iain was out, she said; he'd gone to help his father with the fishing nets.

'Could I come over?' asked Alex. 'I lent Iain a book and I need to have it back. It's important.'

'Of course,' said Iain's mother. 'Come right over.'

Iain lived further along the shore, about fifteen minute's cycle ride away. Alex was winded when he arrived. He dropped his bike on the grass at the side of the house and took a few deep breaths before going in.

'His books will all be up in his room,' said Iain's mother. 'Do you just want to go up and take a look yourself? His room'll be in a right mess, mind.'

Alex didn't mind. He dashed up the stairs. Iain's mother had been right: the room was in a mess, with the bed unmade and clothes everywhere. *Cue for Treason* was not in the bookshelves. He hunted around and as a last resort looked under the bed. And there it was.

He pulled it out. Iain had been using the slip of thin white paper as a bookmark. It protruded visibly between two pages, about halfway through the book.

'All right, Alex?' called up Iain's mother from below.

'All right,' he called back down. 'I've found it.'

He drew out the slip of paper.

'*A search, a journey, and something sharp and bright.*'

FIFTEEN

MAY 1918
FLIGHT FROM ST PETERSBURG

*I*t was the month of May now and Natasha, opening her window, was conscious of spring in the air. She longed to get out into the country and smell the fresh grass and the blossom. Once upon a time, they had had a dacha, a country house set in woods where they had spent their summers, but that had been confiscated by the Bolsheviks. They were like prisoners cooped up in this city house. Uncle Leo had said they would have to leave St Petersburg, but first of all plans had to be laid and of these she knew nothing. If she asked questions she was told she would find out when the time came. And of course she must not even breathe any of this in front of Lena.

When she went downstairs she saw Lena deep in conversation with a man on the doorstep. He was dressed like a peasant. Natasha wondered if he might have food for sale. In the old days, the peasants had brought their food to the back gate, but not now.

Lena said something to the man and closed the door. She had a piece of paper in her hand and she was frowning.

'Is your mother in the salon?' she asked Natasha.

'I think so.'

Lena went ahead of Natasha into the salon. She entered without knocking. Eva was with her sister-in-law, Marie, and her child, Kyril. The two women broke off their conversation as Lena entered.

'I have to go back to my village for a few days, Madame,' said Lena. 'A messenger has brought me news that my mother is seriously ill and may be dying.' She had gone back only once to her village in all the years that Natasha had known her. She always said it was a miserable place and she hated going there.

'I'm sorry to hear that, Lena,' said Eva, rising from her chair. 'But you must go at once, of course. Is there any way in which we can help you?'

Natasha thought her mother sounded strangely sprightly. Perhaps she was just pleased at the thought of Lena's absence for a few days.

'I shall have to get a permit to travel.'

'You of all people should be able to manage that!' The princess smiled at Lena.

Natasha was worried. Her mother should be careful. She had been hinting that Lena could get what she wanted and that she was in favour with the authorities, which they suspected she was.

Lena, however, was too preoccupied with her forthcoming trip to take notice of such innuendoes. She would travel by train part of the way, then she'd have to find a cart to transport her the last few miles. Trains were infrequent and slow when they did get going. It would take her a whole day to reach her village.

'I shall go tomorrow. I can't delay any longer.'

'You must carry plenty of food with you,' insisted

Eva. 'I don't suppose you will find any en route. And you will want a change of clothing. I expect we can find you a suitable travelling bag for your things.' She went without delay and sought out a handsome leather bag and a fine wool travelling cloak in royal blue. She brought them back downstairs. 'This shade of blue should suit you, Lena.'

Natasha looked again at her mother in surprise. She seemed to be taking delight in offering these things to Lena. Something was going on that she did not understand.

Lena allowed the cloak to settle around her shoulders. She stroked the material and smiled. 'This will do very well.' She eyed herself in the gilt-framed mirror on the salon wall. All round the walls there were empty black-edged rectangles where paintings used to hang. They, like much of their jewellery, had been confiscated by the Red Guard. They had rummaged through the house, taking away everything of value that they could lay their hands on. 'I think you are right,' agreed Lena, 'the colour suits me.'

She took the cloak and the bag to her room and then went out to see about her travel permit and a train ticket.

'I thought that was your favourite cloak, Mama,' said Natasha. 'I'm surprised you've given it to Lena.' For Lena would never return it, they knew that.

'What does an old cloak matter, Natasha? There are more important things in life.'

The front door opened and Leo came in carrying his doctor's bag. He raised his eyebrows in an enquiring way at his sister. She nodded. 'Everything's fine,' she told him. 'Going according to plan.'

'Good,' he said, and carried on into the salon to join his wife and son.

'Come upstairs with me, Natasha, love,' said her mother.

They went up to her room and she closed and locked the door behind them. She opened the cupboard and took out a carpet bag. It had a well-travelled air to it.

'I think it probably looks scruffy enough. Though we could dirty it up a little more.'

'But why?'

'We don't want to attract attention, that's why. Take it to your room, Natasha, and pack a few things, but not too many. It mustn't be too heavy for you to carry.'

'Where are we going?'

'Never mind where! It's enough for you to know that we *are* going. We shall leave in the morning after Lena has gone and is out of the way.'

'How did you know she would be going to her village?' Natasha frowned. 'Is her mother not ill then?'

'She may be, she may not. Who knows? She's elderly.'

'But the messenger? Did Uncle Leo send him?'

'Don't ask questions, Natasha! Better not.'

'But it doesn't seem fair that Lena should think her mother might be dying when she's not.'

'Natasha, they say all is fair in love and war. This is war. If we don't get out of here soon it's likely that we shall all end up in prison or Siberia. Lena would not hesitate to help send us there. Uncle Leo is sure she is in the employ of the Secret Police. And they show no mercy to anyone.'

Natasha was silenced. She knew that what her mother had said was true. No mercy had been shown to her grandfather. He had been given no chance to defend himself. He had been shot one morning at dawn without ever seeing his family again.

'So,' said her mother, 'in the morning be ready. Dress warmly but put on your oldest clothes.' She went back to the cupboard and brought out two coarse grey shawls. She gave one to Natasha. 'Wear this over your head. As I said, we must attract as little attention as possible. Our journey is not going to be easy.'

That evening, in her room, Natasha looked at her belongings. What to take, what to leave? She could not carry much, since it had to fit the carpet bag and no more. From the wall above her bed she unhooked the ikon of the Virgin Mary with child, which she prayed to every night before sleeping. It would go with her to protect and console her.

She then put in her sewing basket, but realized at once that it was too awkward and would occupy too much space. Sadly she lifted it out. Her jewelled thimble though, given to her at her christening, would not cause a problem, nor would her amethyst necklace. She would wear her locket she decided, the one with a picture of her mother and father, taken on their wedding day. She slipped it round her neck, under her dress, so that it would not be seen. Next to go into the bag was her small lacquered, beautifully decorated musical box, another christening gift. It had a sweet, melodious tone and when she felt low, she would wind it up and listen to its soft tinkle.

Now for her clothes. She chose a dark blue woollen dress, a couple of changes of underwear and stockings, a warm nightgown, and two pairs of stout shoes. They might have to do a lot of walking. She had no idea how they were going to travel. Their carriages had of course gone long ago.

There was no more room left in the bag. She looked at all the other things she would have liked to have taken and would have to leave behind: books, dolls, her scarlet velvet cloak, her best green velvet dress. She closed the bag and put it under the bed, as her mother had instructed. It was lucky that she did for no sooner had she done so than there came a sharp knock on the door and Lena's voice said, 'Open the door, Natasha. I want to speak to you.'

Natasha had locked the door. Her fingers trembled as they fumbled with the key. What if Lena had found out about their plans? What if she had discovered that the message brought to her was false?

Lena came in and sat herself down on the edge of the bed.

'I want you to keep an eye on the kitchen for me, Natasha. You are a smart girl. You will adjust well to the new life here. Your mother and aunt are useless when it comes to anything practical. It is a wonder they can even dress themselves! I am going to give you the key of the food cupboard.' She passed it over. 'Make sure that no one takes more than their share. If they try to, tell them that I shall report them for disorderly conduct. Understand?'

Natasha nodded. She weighed the heavy key in the palm of her hand.

'And now I must go to bed.' Lena stood up. 'I have an early start and a long day ahead of me.'

Natasha was sure that the day ahead of them would

also be long. She took some time to fall asleep and when she did she dreamt that they were travelling in single file across a vast plain without a horizon. When her mother knocked on her door at first light she found it difficult to surface.

'Natasha, quickly, get up!' called her mother in a low, urgent voice.

She jumped out of bed and hastily washed and dressed. Opening the window shutters she saw a grey mist hanging over the Neva. A black coal barge passed by, gliding slowly and soundlessly. It was empty of coal.

Her mother was waiting in her room, dressed in a long dark coat, with the grey shawl draped over her head and shoulders. In her hand she held a sword.

'Mother,' cried Natasha, 'what are you doing?'

'It's your father's ornamental sword, Natasha. He wore it on formal occasions. I had kept it hidden from the Red Guard. And Lena.'

'But you can't take it with you.'

'No,' her mother agreed sadly, 'of course not.'

'What will you do with it?'

'I shall throw it into the river.' She picked up a carpet bag from the floor, one similar to Natasha's. 'We must get on our way. Lena left an hour ago.'

'What about Uncle Leo? And Aunt Marie and Kyril?'

'They have already left. We shall meet up with them later.'

'And Stepan and Pyotr?' Natasha hated the idea of leaving them behind. They had been two good and trusty servants.

'I know, I feel sorry about them too. But they

couldn't come with us. We'd be too many. I've left an envelope with some money for them, all we could afford, and a note to say thank you.'

They crept down the stairs, making as little noise as possible. The house was silent and still except for the lone cry of a baby in an upper room. They heard a door open somewhere and froze. A moment later they heard it shut again and they went on down into the hall below. Natasha took the key of the food cupboard from her pocket and laid it on a side table. She did not want the lodgers to be deprived of food for the day. They would have to fight it out amongst themselves.

Natasha and her mother paused for a moment to look up, sensing it would be the last time they would see their home. They then let themselves out into the deserted street, closing the heavy door behind them. After giving a quick glance to right and left, Princess Eva crossed the road and dropped her husband's sword into the river Neva. With a flash of silver it was gone, into the dark grey waters.

SIXTEEN

SHARP AND BRIGHT

*A*lex put *Cue for Treason* in his saddlebag and cycled home, clipping the corners rather sharply. He couldn't wait to get back to show his father the latest clue. When he turned in at the gate he saw a strange car sitting outside the front door.

His father was in the drawing room with a woman he had never seen before.

'Alex, this is Mrs Munro. She's an expert on antiques.'

'Hello, Alex,' said the woman cheerfully.

'Mrs Munro has come to value our antiques. Would you show her round?'

Alex conducted Mrs Munro upstairs and downstairs and she dutifully recorded every piece of furniture and every clock and every picture in her book.

'You've got some pretty nice stuff,' she observed. 'Worth quite a lot. You've probably never realized that?'

'We've never thought about it.'

In the sitting room her eye was taken straight away by the sewing basket. She went to it and lifted the lid.

'That belongs to my sister, Sonya.'

Mrs Munro lifted out the thimble. 'Now this is a little beauty. And valuable.'

'That belongs to my sister as well.'

'My instructions were to value everything of worth.'

'But Mr Malenkov *knows* it belongs to Sonya.'

'Alex is right,' said Duncan. 'And some things in this house are ours. Even some things of worth.'

Mrs Munro hesitated for a moment, then she put the thimble back and closed the lid of the box. She wasn't interested in the sitting-room furniture and only made a note of the two Persian rugs that Cousin Boris had fancied.

Finally, she closed the book and stowed it away in her briefcase. She thanked Alex and his father and departed.

They retreated to the library and Alex read out the clue he'd found in *Cue for Treason*.

'"*A search, a journey, and something sharp and bright.*"'

'A lot of books must be about searches,' Duncan reflected.

'And journeys. *Gulliver's Travels*. Aren't there arrows and spears in that?'

'You're right. Better take a look.'

Alex didn't take long to find the book. It was an old edition with thin tissue-like pages protecting the illustrations. He had to go through it page by page since a piece of paper might cling to the thin tissue and not easily fall out. He found nothing.

'Let's press on,' said Duncan. '*Travels with a Donkey*? No, that doesn't seem right.'

Alex checked it out anyway, just to make sure. He drew another blank.

'Something sharp and bright,' said Duncan. 'Let's think about that. What is sharp and bright?'

'A knife?'

'How about a sword?'

'*The Silver Sword*!' Alex jumped up. 'It's a story about children who go on a long journey searching for their lost parents!'

He found the book easily. *The Silver Sword* by Ian Serraillier. And in the middle of it there was a slip of paper. He drew it out.

'*"Another difficult journey, this time involving four-legged creatures."*'

SEVENTEEN

MAY 1918
THE START OF THEIR JOURNEY

They sat huddled in the cabin of the barge, the grey shawls wrapped around their heads. It was stuffy in the small space with so many people crowded together. As well as Natasha and her mother there was the bargee's wife and her five children of assorted ages. The children looked hungry and listless. They leant against their mother, who from time to time cast a sullen glance at the two passengers under lowered eyelids. She had not spoken even when they had greeted her, obviously resenting their presence there. They could not blame her.

After leaving the house they had walked along the embankment to a landing stage a little further down the river. The barge, which normally carried timber, but now had a cargo of only a few bits of scrap, had been waiting for them. The bargee had told them to jump aboard and they had immediately gone down below. Leo had made all the arrangements. He had a lot of friends amongst people he had helped in the past.

One of the children started to cough. It was a raw, convulsive cough, and his nose was running freely. Another was grizzling. Their mother ignored them both. Natasha let her shawl slip back a little from her face and loosened her coat. She could feel beads of sweat breaking out on her forehead.

Suddenly they were jolted forward as the boat lurched to a halt. Natasha looked with alarm at her mother. They had not expected to stop so soon. They heard voices above and cocked their heads, straining to listen. Now footsteps sounded overhead; heavy, clumping footsteps. There seemed to be more than one pair. The ceiling was so low that if they were to stretch up their hands they would feel the vibrations. The barge was rocking slightly. Natasha pulled the shawl back around her head, tucking escaping strands of her long fair hair well out of sight.

'You must hide.' The bargee's wife came to life, pushing the children aside so that she could get to her feet. She was a tall thin woman and there was scarcely room for her to straighten up in the cabin. 'It sounds like the river police.' She lifted a pile of sacks in the corner. 'Here! Make haste!'

Natasha and her mother scrambled underneath the sacks. They were old and filthy and Natasha felt her nose begin to prickle with the smell. But she must not sneeze! She must *not*.

The door to the cabin opened, bringing with it a blast of cold air, and a rasping voice demanded, 'Who is down below?'

'My wife,' said the bargee. 'And our children.'

Natasha pinched her nose between her thumb and forefinger. The man was coming down into the cabin. She felt the floor sway.

'You have a lot of children.'

'Yes, sir. Five in all.'

92

'You have no cargo down here?'

'None. Only what you see on the deck.'

'And those sacks?'

Natasha sucked in her breath.

'Just a pile of old sacks. Fairly stinking they are too. I've been meaning to get rid of them. They're left from the days when I used to carry full loads.'

There was a pause and then the harsh voice said, 'All seems to be in order. You may proceed.'

Natasha and Eva remained underneath the sacks until the visitors had gone and the barge was moving again. The bargee put his head into the cabin and called, 'All clear.'

They crawled out of their hiding place. It would take a long time to rid their hair and clothes of the smell of the sacking.

Some time later, the barge stopped again, which was a great relief to Natasha. She had been feeling sick. The bargee came down and told them to follow him up on to the deck. Emerging into the fresh air, they saw that they had left St Petersburg behind. Looking back, they could just make out the glimmer of its golden spires and domes against the intense blue of the sky. At least they had been blessed with a fine day for their escape. The mist of early morning had evaporated.

'It's beautiful, isn't it?' said Eva, a small catch in her voice. Natasha slid her hand into her mother's.

'I think you know where to go next?' said the bargee.

Eva nodded. 'I cannot thank you enough for your kindness. Here is something you might sell.' She put a gold watch into his hand.

'But, Madame,' he protested.

'Take it, please. You have done us a great favour and put yourself at risk.'

'It was the least I could do for the good doctor. He saved the life of our youngest child. But thank you. And safe journey!'

As he handed them down on to the path, a water rat crossed in front of them and then vanished into the depths of the dark water. Natasha shivered a little.

'Goodbye,' they said to the bargee. 'We won't forget you.'

'Go quickly,' he said.

In spite of the brightness of the day, a cool wind was coming off the river. They put up the collars of their coats. Further along the bank a man was fishing. There appeared to be no one else around. But one never knew whether even the fisherman could be a spy.

'It's a terrible thing when one comes to suspect everybody,' said Eva with a sigh. 'Let's go then, Natasha. We must take the first turning on the right.'

It took them into a street of shabby, old wooden houses. Many of the windows were shuttered though the shutters were splintered and broken. Paint was peeling from doors and window frames. The small patches of ground that passed as gardens were overgrown and littered with rubbish. A mangy dog rooted around in amongst them. A strange eerie silence hung overall. It had the effect of making them look over their shoulders.

'People are afraid to go out, I expect,' said Eva. 'We want the first street on the right. And the third house on the left-hand side.'

It was a low, run-down dwelling, like all the others, and it looked deserted. They glanced about before going up the two steps into the sagging porch. Eva knocked.

Immediately, the door was opened.

'Come in, please,' said a bearded man, dressed in a peasant smock and baggy trousers.

They went into a small room where Leo sat with his wife and son. He sprang up to embrace them.

'Thank goodness! I've been anxious. No one saw you leave the house?'

'Not as far as we know,' said Eva.

'They must be missing us by now though,' said Natasha.

'They won't do anything, not with Lena away,' said Leo. 'They will stay in the house and mind their own business. They might well think you've been taken away by the Secret Police.'

'Would you like some food?' A woman came from a room at the rear carrying a tray on which was set some black bread and a pitcher of jam diluted in water. She wore a peasant skirt and a kerchief on her head.

The travellers ate and drank, urged on by Leo, who said that they would have to take nourishment when and where they found it from now on.

The man with the beard brought out an envelope from a dresser drawer. 'These are your new identity cards and travel documents. Your name until you leave Russia will be Kolkov. And you, Madame, will have the first name of Nadia. Natasha, you will become Katya.'

Natasha took the forged card which would give her a new identity. Katya Kolkova.

'Remember if you are stopped to give the correct name.'

'I am Katya Kolkova,' Natasha repeated inside her head and wondered if she would be able to answer without stumbling.

The woman lifted some garments from a chair. 'Please will you take off your coats and put on these instead. You have to look like peasants who have not much money.'

'But these are not our best coats,' protested Natasha. 'Won't they do?'

'They are still too good for peasants.'

They gave up their wool coats and put on the cheap, thinner ones. But it was almost May and summer should not be long in coming.

'And your shoes,' said the woman. She had a collection of old boots for them to try on. Natasha found a pair that fitted her not too badly. She was beginning to feel like someone else, a completely different girl.

Their bags were next to go and were replaced with grubby canvas sacks.

'These clothes are much too good quality for peasant people,' said the woman, exchanging their spare underwear and nightwear for coarser versions. 'And the musical box, Natasha.' She shook her head. 'I'm afraid you can't take that. If anyone searches your bag they will want to know how you came to have such an expensive toy.'

Natasha wondered what they would do with their things after they left. Sell them? Perhaps this was a good way for the two of them to get hold of other people's possessions. How terrible of her to think such thoughts! Here she was suspecting the very people who were helping them. Uncle Leo must know them well enough to trust them.

Her mother had some jewels in her bag. 'I brought them so that we would have something to sell.'

'Hide them on your person then, Madame. And you, Natasha, keep your necklace well hidden.'

Natasha and her mother stood in the middle of the room in their new clothes, transformed.

'You'll do,' said Leo, who had changed before they came, as had Marie and Kyril.

The bearded man had been keeping watch at the window. 'The cart is here,' he said. 'Come!'

They followed him into the street. The cart was a covered wagon. The driver sat on his box holding the horse's reins loosely in his hands. He wore a wide-brimmed hat and a long coat. He did not turn his head to look at them, but continued to stare straight ahead.

'Your house in St Petersburg has been burned down,' the bearded man instructed them. 'You are going back to your village to stay with relatives. Many people are returning to their villages. The police are pleased enough to see them go. There isn't enough food in the city.'

They said quick goodbyes and the travellers climbed into the back of the wagon. The carter cracked his whip. They were off.

They travelled slowly. The cart wheels rumbled and lurched along pot-holed minor roads. Kyril's mother held on tightly to him. There was little traffic. They passed a number of people trudging along on foot carrying bundles. Fleeing like themselves, it seemed. Twice their horse came to an abrupt halt and stood stock-still in the road. For a few minutes it looked as if he might remain there for the rest of the day, munching grass from the verge. After some cajoling, he eventually made a move.

They had travelled about ten miles when they were met by another cart that would take them on.

'We must cover our tracks as far as possible,' said Leo. 'It is best not to have total trust in anyone.'

'Even the man and woman in the house?' asked Natasha.

'As far as I know, they are reliable. But if the police were to come and question them and put pressure on them?' He shrugged. 'Who can tell? Who can tell what any of us would do under such circumstances? It is best that each person we encounter does not know the next stage of our journey.'

The second cart had smoother wheels and a livelier horse. It clopped along briskly, considering the load it pulled.

'I hope we'll make better time now,' said Leo. 'We must get to our destination before nightfall. It would not be safe to be out on the roads after dark.'

The sun had long since disappeared behind grey, leaden clouds and before they had gone far on this stage of the journey the rain descended. It came down in torrents that the canvas roofing of the cart was inadequate to repel. Soon the travellers were wet through.

They held on to one another as the cart swung wide on a sharp bend. Natasha's shawl slipped from her head.

'Whoa!' cried the carter, reining in his horse.

Up ahead was a roadblock.

EIGHTEEN

ANOTHER JOURNEY

"*'Another difficult journey, this time involving four-legged creatures.'*'

'Well, we know it's not *Travels with a Donkey*,' said Duncan. 'So we can rule that out.'

'Anyway, it says "creatures",' Alex pointed out.

'That's true. And Natasha would be precise about that, I'm sure.'

Lots of people must have travelled with horses, they concluded. There were a number of travel books on the shelves, but most of them Sonya or Alex would not be expected to know. And so far, all the books had been ones that they had read, or in the case of *War and Peace*, heard of.

'There's *Don Quixote*,' said Duncan. 'He had great adventures with Sancho Panzo and they must have had mules or horses.'

Alex found it on the shelf, but there was nothing inside.

One thing that the treasure hunt was doing was making them forget about Sonya's condition for periods of time. And that was good, said Duncan, for they couldn't dwell on it all the time. That would only make them morbid and they had to keep their spirits up.

Anna phoned while they were thinking about journeys and they asked her if she could think of any that might fit the clue.

She sighed. 'I'm afraid my brain doesn't seem to be functioning properly these days. I can't even seem to concentrate enough to read. I just sit here by Sonya's bedside in a kind of coma myself.'

They had felt that was happening to her these last few days and that was why they were trying to interest her in their treasure hunt.

'You must try to go out,' urged Duncan. 'You need the exercise and fresh air. Maybe we should come down?'

'No, no, what's the point?' Anna sighed again. 'Nothing new is happening here. Our Sleeping Beauty just lies, hour after hour. We might need a prince to come and waken her! Or a miracle,' she added quietly.

They were depressed after they rang off.

'I'm worried about your mother,' said Duncan. 'I wish I could go down there and relieve her. I would, if only I weren't so useless, stuck in this stupid chair!'

It was not often that he railed against his disability. But it was understandable that he should sometimes. Anna had talked to them about that after his injury.

'You're not useless, Dad,' said Alex. 'You make great soup.'

Duncan's face relaxed into a grin. 'Glad I'm appreciated.'

'Let's get on with our hunt,' said Alex. 'If we could find the will that would be one thing solved for us.'

'It certainly would!'

The phone rang again and Alex answered it. This time it was Mr Hatton-Flitch on the line. 'I was just phoning to enquire about your sister.'

Alex told him that there was nothing new to report.

'Oh dear, I am so sorry to hear that. You will keep me informed, won't you, if there is any change? By the way, I just thought we'd let you know that we're expecting to get confirmation from the court in a week or two.'

Alex put down the receiver, feeling as if vultures were out there waiting to pick over their bones.

'Come on, lad,' urged his father. 'Journeys! What other ones do you know? With animals?'

Alex frowned. He seemed to think there had been a book about animals going on a long journey. 'Across Canada, wasn't it? A couple of cats and a dog were involved, something like that. But I can't remember the title or who wrote it.'

He scanned the shelves. It took a few minutes, but eventually he gave a whoop of triumph and reached up to pull out *The Incredible Journey* by Sheila Burnford.

'Fingers crossed, Dad!'

Alex flicked through the pages and found a slip of paper.

'Well?' Duncan was waiting impatiently.

'Here it is!' Alex read out the clue, '"*A small abode in an open place.*"'

NINETEEN

*T*he rain had stopped, but the wind was piercingly cold. They stood in the roadway, shivering in their wet clothes, keeping their eyes averted from the two policemen who had ordered them down from the cart.

'Identity cards!'

They handed the cards over and the men scrutinized them. Natasha moved closer to her mother.

'Your name?' they demanded of Leo. He answered calmly and surely. They fired the question at Marie and then Natasha's mother. The two women were also able to keep their nerve and did not hesitate before replying, though there was a slight tremor in Eva's voice. The men turned to face Natasha, ignoring Kyril.

'And you. What is your name?'

'Katya Kolkova,' she said calmly. She felt amazingly calm.

They looked again at Leo. 'So, where are you going?'

Leo named a village some distance away. He went on to tell how their house in the city had been set alight by a mob and had burnt to the ground. 'We have nowhere to live so we are going back to stay with our relatives.'

'What work will you do there?'

'Anything. Labouring. I will work on the land if I can.'

His hands did not look like those of a labourer or farm worker. They were too white and smooth. As if he had suddenly become aware of that himself, he stuck them into the pockets of his baggy coat.

The men seemed to hesitate for a moment as if they were not totally happy with the answers they'd received. Then one of them took out his watch and said, 'It's late. We should be back at the barracks.'

'We'd better take a look at their luggage first,' said the other. 'Fetch your bags from the cart. Bring them here.'

They did as they were told, laying their bags out in the road for inspection. The men rifled quickly through them, letting clothes spill on to the road. A teddy bear landed in a puddle and Kyril began to cry. His mother comforted him and his father reached for the bear, but one of the policemen barked, 'Leave it!' He picked it up himself and examined it closely, looking perhaps for concealed jewels or something of that nature. Then he tossed it back to the child.

As he reached for Natasha's bag, the rain started again in earnest. The man glanced up at the sky and swore and only gave the contents at the top a quick check.

'Let's go,' said his companion. 'It's past supper time. There'll be no food left.'

The policeman shoved Natasha's bag aside. 'All right then. On your way!'

They gathered up their possessions and clambered back into the wagon to resume their journey.

They travelled till the sun was sinking in the western sky, by which time they were exhausted. Their minds felt dulled from the rumbling of the wheels and their bones ached from the pitching and rolling of the cart. Their clothes stuck to them in a damp mass.

They passed the night in a remote farmhouse, where they were expected. The farmer and his wife said little and kept their names to themselves. The travellers' wet clothes were spread in front of the kitchen stove. After a meal of bread and soup they lay down on a bed of furs on the floor and slept until the cocks crowing at dawn wakened them. A new cart and a new driver awaited them. And so they journeyed on.

And then, one morning, after many long, weary days on the road, they emerged from their overnight lodging to find the road was empty. There was no sign of a cart.

'We are going to have to walk for the next part of our journey,' Leo told them.

It was a relief to be on foot rather than being tossed about in the back of a cart. For a while their route took them along a riverbank, whose edge was curtained by a line of willows. After a kilometre or two, they veered off on to a track leading into a birch wood. The path under the trees was soft underfoot and the sun shone through the branches, making the fresh green leaves glitter. Overhead, numerous birds chattered and warbled. For the first time since leaving home, Natasha felt that it might be possible to smile again. The morning was beautiful. The wood felt safer too than the open road. Here, they were sheltered from the curious gaze of passers-by. Not that anyone would take them for an aristocratic family now, they were so bedraggled and stained. They looked like any other homeless peasant family on the move, carrying their canvas sacks.

Emerging from the wood, they found themselves in open, rolling countryside. They glanced nervously about. In a nearby field, a man was ploughing. Two lumbering oxen pulled the heavy wooden plough. The man lifted his head and Leo called out a greeting.

'Fine morning!'

'It will rain before lunchtime,' the ploughman responded. Looking up, they saw that clouds had started to move in from the west, from the direction of the Baltic Sea.

They pushed on, taking a rutted lane that ran between two fields. They had been steadily moving southward, Natasha realized. Her uncle kept looking at the position of the sun. He had no map on him, would not have dared to carry one. And anyway, tracks such as these would not feature on any map.

'I'm tired,' whined Kyril, when they had gone only a short distance. 'Can't walk any more. My feet hurt.' He plonked himself down on the path.

His father hoisted him up on to his back.

Natasha felt the first spot of rain on her cheek. In a brief time, the sky had turned from a soft blue to a steel grey.

'We'd better shelter,' said Leo, indicating a clump of trees up ahead. By the time they reached it, their clothes were damp again. The downpour proved heavy and the trees, not yet being in full leaf, did not give sufficient cover. When the sun re-emerged they were soaked to the skin.

'We'll catch our death if we go on like this getting repeatedly soaked,' said Marie. Kyril began to cry again. He had been crying at intervals ever since they had left St Petersburg.

'I've got a sore ear.' He clamped his hand over his left ear. He had complained about it before, but no one had had time to pay any attention.

His father examined it. 'It does look a bit red, but I expect the swelling will go down. First thing we've got to do is change our clothes.'

The clothes in their bags were only slightly damp; the canvas had protected them fairly well. They changed and spread their wet clothes out on bushes to dry. Leo said they might as well rest a while and have their lunch.

The meal consisted of bread and water and a piece of hard cheese, but they were glad enough of it and the chance to ease their feet for a while. Kyril ate nothing and continued to complain and his mother to rock him.

'He's in pain, Leo,' she said despairingly. 'Can you do nothing to help him?'

His father took another look at the ear and frowned. 'I don't like the look of it, I have to admit. But there's not a lot I can do. If only we had some heat to put on it.'

'How can we get heat here in the middle of a field?'

'We could ask the man who was ploughing,' suggested Natasha. 'He might let us come into his house.'

'It's a risk,' said Leo.

Kyril cried out sharply again.

'We have to do something!' said his mother.

'All right,' said Leo. 'We'll try him.'

'Can I go with you?' asked Natasha.

'Very well.'

There was no sign of the man in the half-ploughed field. The oxen stood idly by the plough.

'He could be having his lunch,' said Natasha.

Smoke was coming from the chimney of the nearby farmhouse.

'They must have a fire,' she said.

Her uncle nodded. 'Let's go and see.'

It was a small house, looked to be no more than two rooms, but it was in a reasonable state of repair, unlike many that they had seen. A porch screened the front door. They went up the steps and knocked.

The ploughman came out, a piece of bread in his hand. Leo apologized for disturbing his meal and explained their problem. 'If we could just bring the boy into the warm for a few minutes and heat a sock to put against his ear.'

'One moment.' The man went back inside and reappeared almost immediately to say that they could come in. 'But we cannot invite you to stay too long.'

'No, we understand that. But thank you for your kindness.'

Kyril was brought in to the fire and the farmer's wife gave them some salt to put inside a sock, which was then heated beside the stove. The warmth seemed to soothe the pain somewhat. Kyril's eyes closed.

'Poor boy,' said the farmer's wife. 'A sore ear is a terrible thing. It eats into the whole head. I have some herbs that might help. I used them for my son when he was small.'

'Is he grown up now?' asked Natasha.

'Yes, and gone away. He joined the Red Army. The last we heard, he was on the Eastern Front fighting the Whites.'

The news quietened them. But at least the Eastern Front was far away and the son was scarcely likely to walk in at any moment.

The woman mixed the herbs with water and Kyril was persuaded to swallow the bitter mixture. 'It will reduce the fever,' she promised.

They stayed an hour in the house and then they left, the farmer accompanying them back to the lane.

'I am not a political man,' he said. 'I do not mind what colour people are. Red. White. It is all the same to me. As long as they leave me in peace.'

'Thank you.' Leo held out his hand to the man. 'You are a good man.'

'You are not far from the border. Take that track over there and keep going until you come to a stile. Cross that and you will find that you have crossed the border. Good luck!'

They took the track and kept going until they came to a stile.

'So,' said Leo, 'this must be it. The border.'

He paused before he climbed over and then helped the others to cross.

'We are now in Estonia.'

Estonia previously had been part of the Russian Empire, but it was no longer. Russia had been forced to give up the country to Germany. The Great War was still being fought between Germany and the Allied Forces. But the travellers were not thinking of that war, or what it might mean to them. They were looking back at Russia, their homeland.

TWENTY

A SMALL ABODE

'*A* small abode in an open place.'

'I *think* this one should be easy,' said Alex cautiously. 'A small abode could be a little house, couldn't it?'

'It could,' agreed his father.

'I'm going to start by trying *The Little House on the Prairie*. You'd call a prairie an open place, wouldn't you?' Sonya had been especially keen on those books. He couldn't remember who had written them, however. His father had no idea either.

'Still, a title's a good start,' said Duncan.

Alex was already searching. 'I hope Sonya didn't lend this one out to anybody!' He found *The Little House in the Big Woods* first and pulled it out. 'Laura Ingalls Wilder, that's who wrote them. This can't be it though.'

'No, you wouldn't call woods an open place.'

Alex continued his search along the shelves. Two rows from the bottom he pounced. He opened the book and lifted out a piece of paper.

'*That wasn't so bad, was it?*' Natasha had written. '*That was a clue especially for Sonya; Alex might be the one to solve this clue. This nasty item tends to repeat itself. An American invention, I believe, first used in the Civil War. I pity the men who have to operate it, apart from those on the receiving end.'*

TWENTY-ONE

Now that they had left the Red Army behind and were in Estonia, they could relax a little. There was a new force to be wary of here, however: the German army of occupation. Germany might no longer be at war with the Russian Empire, but it had no liking for Russians, suspecting them all of being communist and supporting the Bolsheviks.

'Say nothing,' instructed Leo, 'when there are any soldiers in the vicinity. Let me do the talking.' He could speak some Estonian.

'Why do so many people have to be fighting one another?' asked Natasha. She found it difficult to follow who was at war with whom. 'Does anyone like *us*?'

'If we could get to Paris,' said her uncle, 'we would find friends there.'

Natasha knew Paris was a long way away. She remembered looking at it in her atlas at her happy little school in St Petersburg and thinking that one day she would like to go there. It was said to be beautiful. She had not imagined that she would be travelling like this, on foot, carrying bundles, keeping a wary eye open for possible enemies, dodging into woods whenever army patrols were sighted up ahead.

The days had lengthened and the nights were very short. At home, they had called the shortest summer nights 'white nights'. They slept rough in woods or empty barns. A lot of the farm buildings seemed to have been abandoned; they were in a bad state of repair. The countryside looked sad and neglected.

Leo was carrying money so they were able to buy food in the villages, such as was available. It was mostly bread and hard white cheese and sometimes, if they were lucky, a pitcher of milk. The peasants looked at them with no great interest. There was no shortage of refugees roaming about, many of them Russian.

Kyril still complained of his ear, though it seemed not to have got any worse. He grumped most of the day and was restless at night. His father would sit on the ground rocking him, with his back against a tree trunk. Both father and son had deep shadows underneath their eyes.

'We must go to Tallin,' said Leo. 'I have a friend there, a doctor, who I'm sure will take us in. We studied medicine together. It would be good to shelter in a house for a while and rest up. It would be wonderful!'

'And have a bath?' put in Natasha. She had bracelets of grime around her wrists and her neck must be filthy! They had had to make do with washing in streams and without soap since leaving home. How long ago had that been? Two weeks? Three? She couldn't begin to guess. The days had blurred, one into the other. Time had come to have little meaning. It seemed like a lifetime ago almost, when she and her mother had closed the door of their old home behind them.

As they approached the outskirts of Tallin, Estonia's capital, their nervousness increased. But once they were in the city and mingling with the other throngs of poorly clad people, they realized that they did not stand out. Leo knew the city well enough not to have to ask for directions. He had visited his friend before, had stayed with him on several occasions before the start of the Great War in 1914.

It was a city on the sea, another Baltic port, like St Petersburg, and it had buildings that once had been fine, but had suffered much damage during the German shelling. Rubble lay in the roadway. Half-demolished houses stood open to the elements. Machine guns were still mounted at crossroads and other strategic points.

They passed nervously by. Natasha hoped Leo's friend's house would still be standing.

'This is it,' he said. 'This is the street.'

They turned into a broad, pleasant suburban street. War did not seem to have touched it greatly. The trees in the gardens were coming into leaf and the buildings were intact. Leo brought them to a halt in front of a large detached brick house.

The gate stood open. They went up the path in single file and saw that the garden had been neglected; weeds flourished and the grass grew wild. Would there be anyone at home? The place did not have the feel of being occupied. Natasha supposed though, that nobody would have had time during the war to cut grass and pull out weeds. And, as in St Petersburg, all the servants might have run away.

Her uncle knocked on the door and they waited on the steps behind him. For a moment, it seemed that their fears might prove well founded. Nothing happened. Kyril started to cry. Leo knocked again and after a short pause they heard a movement within and then the door opened a few centimetres. A woman holding a baby peered out at them.

Leo asked for his friend. The woman shook her head and was about to close the door when he said, 'Wait!' and put his toe over the step. 'Are you sure?'

'There's no one of that name here.'

'But this is his house.'

'He doesn't live here, I tell you. And you can't come in. There are too many here already. All the rooms are full. There must be twenty of us in all.'

Leo let her close the door. The house had obviously been taken over by refugees. And as for his friend and his family? They would possibly never find out. That was the way it was in wartime.

'We shall have to make our way to the railway station,' he decided, 'and see if we can get a train to Riga. We can't walk all the way there.' He also knew some people who lived in that city, though he would no longer count on finding them at home.

The station, when they reached it, was in a state of chaos. Finding an official proved difficult to start with and when they did, he could give them little information. He shrugged and waved vaguely at a platform. They bought tickets and sat down on the ground to wait. After three hours, a train steamed in and they piled on board with what seemed like ten thousand others.

It was hot in the carriage and the stench of close-packed bodies was suffocating. One toilet served all the carriages and after the first half-hour it was in a disgusting state, foul-smelling and overflowing on to the floor. Natasha did not want to use it, but eventually she was forced to as she thought her bladder might burst. She had to hold her nose to stop herself gagging. There was no lock on the door. Her mother remained outside to keep other desperate travellers at bay.

The train chugged slowly along, stopping at times as if to take a rest and gather strength to continue. Hours passed. Natasha stood in the corridor with her uncle, watching the countryside unfold. More birch woods. Some small farms. Wild flowers growing in bright rashes in the hedgerows. A few cows. Her mind felt dulled. She felt almost as though she could have fallen asleep standing up. At some point they crossed the border into Latvia, though they were not aware when exactly they did so. Another border, another country.

Latvia was also under German command. They became aware of that as soon as they arrived in Riga. The grey uniforms of the German army were much in evidence in the station. The family was stopped at a barrier by two soldiers demanding to see their papers. They handed over their documents, the ones that had been forged and given to them on the day that they had left home. At this stage, it would have been better if they had had their original ones showing that they came from an aristocratic family. A count would not be suspected of being a communist.

'Russians, eh?'

'White Russians,' said Leo. 'We have fled from the Bolsheviks.'

'Oh yes?' The soldier looked him over, from the top of his dishevelled hair to the frayed boots on his feet. 'And I'm the King of England!'

'I can only give you our word.' Leo could not tell them that he was Count Malenkov and his sister Princess Eva Denisova, for that would reveal that they were carrying forged papers.

'Where are you going in Riga?'

'To a friend's house.'

They asked for the address and, with some hesitation, Leo gave it to them. He could not have risked giving a false address and it seemed unlikely they would follow it up.

'All right then. You may go.'

They went into the streets. The capital of Latvia lay half in ruins. Shrapnel, rubble, lumps of twisted metal and shards of broken glass littered the pavements. The city, like Tallin, had been heavily shelled by the Germans before they'd occupied it. Leo stood in the middle of the pavement, appalled by what he saw.

'It was such a lovely city!'

'Your friends may no longer be here,' said Natasha.

'No, they may not. They might have gone into the country to escape the shelling. We have to be prepared for that.'

The hour was late, close to midnight. There was no sign of civilians in the shadowy streets, only soldiers. The family felt conspicuous and were glad of the poor lighting as they picked their way through the rubble. Glass crackled under their feet and Eva almost twisted her ankle on a fallen girder. Natasha took her arm. Leo was having a problem finding his way.

'Half the landmarks are gone,' he muttered. 'But the apartment is round here somewhere, I know it is. I visited Karl here several times.' They had also been fellow students at the University of St Petersburg.

'What are we to do, Leo?' Marie burst suddenly into tears. 'We can't go on like this much longer.'

'We have no choice, dear.' He put his arm round his wife's shoulders. 'If we don't go on we lie down and die.'

She dried her eyes on a rag. 'You're right, of course.'

'I have a feeling it's just round this next corner.'

It was! The building still stood, so at least that was encouraging, and the bottom door was open.

'They're one flight up.'

They climbed the stairs to the first floor and Leo rang the bell.

Karl's wife, Andra, opened the door on a chain, which she unhooked on recognizing Leo. She embraced him warmly.

'Karl?' asked Leo.

'He was killed in the shelling. One night he left the hospital where he was working and got caught in the machine-gun fire. Half of our friends are dead.' Tears welled up in Andra's eyes.

'Ours too.' Leo shook his head. 'You have our deepest sympathy, Andra.'

'Come in, please,' she said.

Andra had four children, all of whom were under the age of seven. Living also in the apartment was her sister with her three small children. Her husband had been another casualty of the war. It was fortunate that the flat was spacious.

'We help one another,' said Andra. 'You are welcome to stay for a while, Leo, if you don't mind all sleeping in one room.'

'A room will be a luxury,' Eva reassured her. 'We are most grateful.'

'I have little food.' Andra was apologetic.

'We shall find our own,' promised Leo.

'My uncle is very good at finding things,' said Natasha.

'And you are very good at helping to find them!' he returned.

The family settled in. Leo was taken on at a city hospital and although his wages were not high, they were enough to feed them and to help Andra's family too. Doctors were scarce in the city and therefore much in demand. Leo worked long hours and came home exhausted. Soldiers were returning from the war with horrifying injuries. They could be seen limping through the city streets in tattered, blood-stained uniforms, with soles flapping from their boots or with no boots at all, their feet raw and suppurating. Some collapsed and lay where they had fallen until a cart came to take them away. Many had to have limbs amputated.

Sometimes Leo took Natasha with him to the wards. She was thinking that she might like to be a doctor when she grew up. Whilst the sight of so much blood and suffering distressed her, it did not make her want to run away. She wanted to do something. She took water round the beds and helped the patients to take small sips. She talked to the men and asked them about their homes and families. One of them called her 'our little angel', which made her blush. The name caught on.

'She's too young to see such things, Leo,' her mother protested. 'She's not thirteen yet.'

'She has seen a great deal. Unfortunately. Her childhood has been shattered early. But that is how it is. She copes well, she is strong. Let her come with me, Eva. She wants to come.'

Sometimes Natasha went out walking with her mother. They liked to go down to the harbour to look at the sea. Riga was another port on the Baltic, like Tallin and St Petersburg. They would stand gazing at the sea and imagine setting sail on a boat that would bear them northward, back up the coast, to St Petersburg.

'Will we ever go back, do you think, Mama?' asked Natasha.

'Who knows?' said Eva sadly.

They had grown closer since their flight from St Petersburg. Before the revolution, their lives had been lived much more separately, with Eva going out and about with her society friends and entertaining them in her salon, while Natasha had lived in her own rooms, tended by a nurse in her early years, and later by Lena. That old life seemed far away.

On the eleventh of November, Leo came home to tell them that an armistice had been signed between Germany and the Allies. The Great War was at an end.

'Does that mean we can move on now to Paris?' asked Eva.

'I think so.' Leo sounded cautious. 'They say

though, that the Germans are not going to leave Latvia that easily. But, come the spring, and better weather, we must try to make it.' In the meantime, he was going to put aside part of his wages each month for their travel to France. They would take a train. To even consider walking would be ludicrous. From Latvia they would have to go through Lithuania, then into Poland, and from there into Germany. That would still leave them a long way from Paris. But they would have to move on. They couldn't stay there in Riga for ever, crowding out Andra in her own home.

'We will go in the spring,' Leo told her.

She said they were welcome to stay as long as they needed to. 'Karl would have wished it. He was fond of you, Leo. He talked often about your student days together, of the fun you used to have!'

The days now were short and dark and the first snows of winter fell. Ice formed on the insides of the windows overnight. They were unable to heat the rooms properly. Half the children in the flat were coughing. At the hospital, a few cases of typhoid had cropped up and Natasha could no longer go with Leo. He came home even later at nights and looked grey and thin. His wife fussed over him.

'You will get ill yourself, Leo. You should stay in bed and rest for a day.'

'How can I?'

One night, he didn't come back when expected, although that was not unusual. Marie was worried and kept pulling back the curtain to look out into the night.

'Something has happened to him, I know it has! I feel it.'

'I expect there has been yet another emergency,' said Eva.

But when Leo had not returned by morning, Marie and Natasha set out for the hospital. It was snowing. With shawled heads bent, they faced the blizzard. The city, shrouded in drifting, swirling snow, had the appearance of a ghost city. Little traffic was on the streets and not even the soldiers were in evidence. By the time they reached the hospital they were wet through.

They discovered that the reason Leo had not come home was that he had been taken ill himself and was lying in one of the ward beds. He was delirious and running a high fever. Marie and Natasha were told that they could not see him. It would not be safe for them to do so.

'We fear he has contracted typhoid.'

Leo died later that day.

TWENTY-TWO

THE AMERICAN CIVIL WAR

'"*T*his nasty item tends to repeat itself*",' read Duncan. '"*An American invention, I believe, first used in the Civil War. I pity the men who have to operate it. Alex might be the one to solve this clue.*"'

'I don't know anything about the American Civil War,' said Alex. 'Except that there was one. I know that the North was fighting the South, that's about all.'

'It was a bloody war,' said Duncan. 'But then all wars are. No one knew that better than Natasha.'

Alex frowned. 'Why did Natasha say that I might be the one to solve it?'

'Maybe it was a book that you particularly liked?'

Alex couldn't think of a book involving something to do with the American Civil War.

'What would they have used in the Civil War?' wondered Duncan aloud. 'Muskets, fifes and drums! But none of them would *first* have been used there.'

They didn't have any books set in that war, not that the clue would be intended to imply that. Alex felt a bit bamboozled because he'd been picked out specially.

'Let's think about a nasty item that tends to repeat itself,' said his father. 'If it's nasty it's probably something that can kill. Now a machine gun repeats itself.'

Alex smiled. *The Machine Gunners*! When he'd brought Robert Westall's novel home Natasha had said, 'That's a nasty title!'

'But a good book,' he'd replied.

He found the book quite quickly.

'"*Well done, Alex! The next tale is a revolutionary one and capital in more ways than one.*"'

TWENTY-THREE

RIGA AND PARIS, 1919
JOURNEYING ON

*T*hey were all devastated by Leo's death. His wife had gone into hysterics when she had heard the news.

'We are doomed,' she had cried. 'We cannot survive without him!'

Neither Natasha nor her mother could answer, for the same thought was in their minds. How could they manage without Leo? He had been their leader and their rock. They had looked to him at every turn. It was he who had always known what to do, where to go. It was he who had taken all the decisions. It was he who had earned the money to keep them alive.

Temperatures outside stood below zero and the burial had to be delayed for several days until the cold, hard ground thawed sufficiently to allow the grave diggers to do their work. They were days of misery during which the women moaned and sobbed and the child Kyril clung to Natasha and for once was silent himself. She went about in a state of shock, taking her young cousin with her when she went out into the town to search for food or fuel.

Andra helped her make arrangements for the funeral. They found a Russian Orthodox priest who was willing to conduct a ceremony at the graveside. He came in his hat and cassock with a heavy crucifix hanging against his black chest. The wind ruffled his long white beard. The women stood beside the open grave while the priest swung an incense burner and intoned the last rites of the Orthodox church.

The wind was bitter that day and the soles of their shoes were thin. Going home, Eva felt that the chill had entered her bones. When she reached the apartment she lay down in the bed she shared with Natasha to try to get warm, but she continued to shiver and her teeth chattered uncontrollably. In the night, she developed a high temperature, alarming Natasha, who rose and applied a sponge wrung out in cold water to her mother's forehead. But no matter how many times she chilled the sponge, she found that her mother's forehead remained blistering hot to her cold hand.

She couldn't have typhoid, she couldn't! Please God, Natasha prayed, *please don't let her die!* She prayed in front of her mother's ikon, a small, beautiful painting on wood of the Virgin in blue and gold. Each member of the family had brought their own special ikons with them. They had taken Leo's to the cemetery and left it there to keep guard over his grave and hoped that no one would have the temerity to steal it. Stealing was rife in the city.

At first light, Natasha decided to go to the hospital to seek help. She asked Andra to sit with her mother until she returned and then she set out. They *must* help her at the hospital. Surely they must. Leo had given his life to the patients. She ran most of the way, taking care not to slip on the icy pavements. She passed a woman in a long faded evening dress carrying a saucepan. Her face was emaciated and her hair hung down in rats' tails over her bare shoulders. She looked into Natasha's face with unseeing eyes and asked in a toneless voice, 'Have you any food?'

'I'm sorry,' said Natasha and hastened on.

At the hospital, she spoke to a nurse who she had often helped on the wards.

'I wish I could help you, Natasha. But there isn't much we can do. We can't take her in here. The place is full to overflowing, you know that yourself. Give your mother sips of water with a little salt and a little sugar, keep her warm and hope that she will sweat out the fever. That is the best advice I can give you. And to pray!'

'You wouldn't have a spare blanket you could let me have?'

'I don't really have any spare, but I'll give you one. Your uncle was a good man and a kind doctor. There are not so many like him. May the Good Lord be with him!'

Natasha burst into tears. It was the first time that she had cried. The nurse took her in her arms and comforted her and before she left, gave her a small amount of sugar in a bag and some bread and an egg. 'You eat the egg and bread yourself, dear. You must look after yourself and keep your strength up.'

On the way back, Natasha's legs felt as if they were filled with sand. She stood for a moment outside the apartment. She wanted to sit down on the pavement and howl. Instead, she took a deep breath and climbed the stairs. Their room smelt like a sick room. Her mother had turned delirious and was raving and toss-ing in the bed. Andra was there in the room, but fearing that she might become infected herself she was not sitting too close to the bed.

'I have to think of the children,' she said apologetically.

Natasha nodded. 'Of course.' She did not even dare to think that she might be the next one to fall ill. She was aware that it was a possibility, but felt calm about it. What could she do? It was too late now. She had been sleeping close to her mother and she had to tend her, to sponge her head, to hold the cup to her lips. Her aunt, like Andra, was keeping her distance and making sure that Kyril, too, stayed on the other side of the room.

For three days and two nights Eva tossed in delirium and on the third night the fever broke. Natasha dried her with towels and helped her to take small sips of water. Suddenly the patient became still and quiet, and opening her eyes, recognized her daughter. Natasha burst into tears for the second time.

Her mother recovered slowly. After a week she was able to get out of bed and stand, but only for a few minutes. She was exceedingly weak.

'What are we to do?' moaned Marie. 'We can't stay here for ever. Leo would have known what to do.' It was her constant cry.

'We shall go to Paris,' said Natasha. 'When Mama is strong enough.'

'Paris? How can we go to Paris? Do you know how far it is?'

'We shall have to go by train.'

'And how are we to do that? It costs money to go by train.'

'Uncle Leo had some money left.'

'Not enough to pay four fares. And we're having to use some of the money to buy food.'

Natasha realized that no matter what she proposed, her aunt would always have a negative response. She resolved to keep her counsel and to try to devise a way for them to get to France. She looked again at an atlas. It was a daunting prospect, the idea of travelling such a distance. But her uncle had thought they could do it. Thinking of him stiffened her resolve. She began to plan ahead. In the meantime, her mother had to recover her strength and the winter to pass. It was impossible to consider setting out anywhere while the weather was so severe.

Natasha reached her thirteenth birthday.

'Happy birthday, my love,' said her mother, giving her a hug. 'I'm sorry I have no presents to give you. Maybe next year!'

'Next year we shall be in Paris.'

'Paris.' Eva sounded wistful. 'Paris and St Petersburg – my two favourite cities! Your father and I went to Paris for our honeymoon. We took a boat trip down the Seine by moonlight. I am glad I had such a happy time then.'

'You'll have happy times again, Mama. In Paris.'

'Well, we'll see.'

So her mother did not believe her either.

Natasha went one morning to a narrow street in the medieval old town. She had noticed a shop there, a jeweller's, had looked in the window and studied the articles for sale spread out on a dusty velvet cloth. There had not been many. Opening the door, she remembered going into a similar shop in St Petersburg with her mother. This one was low-ceilinged and had a musty smell.

The man behind the counter looked up from the watch he was working on and peered at her through round-rimmed spectacles. 'Yes, young lady?' He spoke in German. It was the language of most traders in the city. The street signs were all in German, which made Latvians like Andra angry. She wanted Latvian to be the main language and said that one day it would be. She wanted her country to be independent.

'You buy jewellery?' asked Natasha. She had learned enough German, as she had Latvian, to be able to converse simply.

'Why, young lady? Do you have something that might interest me?'

She laid her amethyst necklace on the counter. He named a ridiculously low price.

'That is too little,' she said and lifted it up, making as if to leave.

'Wait!' He named another sum, which still she refused.

'You are a very determined young lady.' Eventually he paid her, perhaps not what the necklace was worth, but enough to cover their fares to Paris and to have a little over. She tucked the money away, under their mattress.

The days lengthened and the frosts receded. Eva now felt strong enough to walk in the park and take a little air. She leant on her daughter's arm. Gradually the stark trees began to show signs of life; a few pale-green buds announced the coming of spring.

'It's time for us to go,' said Natasha.

'Go where?' asked her aunt.

'To Paris. Where else?'

'On foot?'

'I have tickets for the train from Riga to Vilnius.' Vilnius was the capital of Lithuania, the third Baltic state that lay to the south of Latvia. 'And money to take us on from there.' Natasha told them that she had sold her necklace. Her mother lamented, but only briefly.

'And where are we to go when we get to Paris?' asked Marie.

'I'm not sure. Uncle Leo knew some people there, didn't he?'

'But we don't know where they live. There, we might have to sleep on the pavement; here, we have a roof over our heads.'

Leo had left no address book; it had not been something he could have brought on the journey, for fear it would fall into the wrong hands.

'Don't come if you don't want to then!' said Natasha, her temper rising. She left the room before she would say anything else. At times her aunt made her want to stamp her foot.

Marie, of course, did go with them. What else could she have done? In the early morning, she trudged along to the station behind them, looking sullen. Kyril took Natasha's free hand. In the other, she carried the bundle that contained all her worldly possessions. They had been sad to say goodbye to Andra; she had been so good to them.

The station was full of German soldiers. They piled on to the Vilnius train when it came in, leaving no room for other passengers. The family had to wait in the station until the middle of the afternoon when they finally managed to board a train. In Vilnius, they slept in the station overnight, waiting for yet another train, which would take them on into Poland.

And so their journey continued, in fits and starts, through Poland and Germany. Most of Europe seemed to be in a state of upheaval after the war. Stations were crowded, trains broke down. Everywhere to be seen were defeated soldiers, some walking with glazed eyes, trying to keep their heads up, others wounded, limping, using crutches to aid their progress with empty trouser legs pinned up, heads bandaged, arms trussed into slings.

Finally, the travellers crossed the border into France and on a fine spring day, when the blossom was out along the banks of the river Seine, they arrived in Paris.

TWENTY-FOUR

A CAPITAL TALE

Alex read the clue out again. '"*The next tale is a revolutionary one and capital in more ways than one.*"'

'Capital could mean an *excellent* tale,' said Duncan. 'On the other hand, it could refer to a capital city. And then there's the revolution.'

'St Petersburg?' said Alex. 'It had a revolution. There must have been revolutions in half the capitals in the world?'

'Indeed. And some of them quite recent! In the Baltic States and other Eastern European countries, for a start.'

'Wasn't there a famous one in Paris a long time ago?'

Duncan nodded. 'At the end of the eighteenth century. That was when they threw out the monarchy and became a republic.'

'And the old women sat knitting at the guillotine watching people getting their heads chopped off?' Alex became excited. 'Hey, didn't Dickens write a book about that?'

'He certainly did. It was called *A Tale of Two Cities*.'

'That fits!' Alex jumped up. 'Capital in more ways than one.'

'Two capitals! Paris and London.'

Alex ran to the bookshelves and ran his finger along the one holding the works of Charles Dickens. He pulled out the book he was looking for and swiftly rifled through it.

'Got it!' He extracted the paper.

'*The next clue is the last one,*' Natasha had written, '*and I am making it easy since you have done well coming this far. You will find it in a receptacle filled with pleasure.*'

'"*A receptacle filled with pleasure*",' repeated Duncan.

'I suppose you could say a lot of books are filled with pleasure.' Alex frowned. 'Natasha might have given us a bit more of a clue. She said it was going to be easy.'

'You don't think she'd make it *too* easy, do you? Let's think about "a receptacle". What do you make of that?'

'Something to put something in.'

'Exactly. What about a box?'

'*A Box of Delights*!' said Alex. 'Who wrote that? I can't remember.'

'John Masefield.'

'I remember Natasha reading it to us when we were quite small. I remember her saying she liked the word "delights".'

'Go on then, take a look!'

Alex found the book without any trouble. He took it down and gave it a gentle shake. Nothing floated out. He flicked through the pages, frowning as he got closer to the end.

'There's nothing here!'

'Are you sure?'

Alex checked one more time.

'We'll just have to think again then,' said his father.

They thought. They couldn't think of any other titles on their shelves with 'box' in it.

Alex went up to his room and switched on his computer. He put in 'receptacle', then brought up the thesaurus. A fairly short list of synonyms was listed and it didn't even include 'box'.

Container

Can

Canister

Bin

Bucket

Package

Alex stared at the screen. Nothing there was very inspiring. What kind of title could you get with 'bucket' or 'canister' in it?

They waited until Anna rang and consulted her.

'We thought it would be *A Box of Delights,* but it wasn't,' said Duncan, who had answered the phone. He listened for a moment, then broke off to say to Alex, 'Your mother says we should have two copies of *A Box of Delights.*'

Alex began to search afresh. His mother stayed on the other end of the phone while he did.

'Tell Mum I can't see it,' said Alex.

Duncan told her. Alex went on looking and double-checking. He was getting good at scanning titles quickly and he had a fair idea now where most things were.

'Is she sure?' he asked his father.

'Are you sure?' asked Duncan into the receiver. He listened again, then looked up at Alex. 'She seems pretty certain about it. One copy was illustrated – that's the one we've found – and the other wasn't. Wait a minute!' Anna was talking to him again. 'She says she thinks it might have gone to the church fête along with a load of other books.'

TWENTY-FIVE

PARIS, 1919
THE MEETING OF NATASHA AND EUGENIE

*T*hey spent their first night in Paris sleeping under one of the bridges that spanned the Seine. They huddled close together for warmth, dozing intermittently. Natasha rose before it was fully light and walked up and down the towpath, flapping her arms about. She felt as stiff as a paving slab, and as cold.

Smudges of pink and pale green and lemon yellow began to nudge into the sky. She faced east to watch the dawn break. It was a spectacular dawn and as she watched, she forgot her stiff limbs and cold feet. The river rippled with the colours reflected from the sky. She turned to see her mother stirring.

'Come and look, Mama!'

Eva joined her. They stood by the water's edge until the sky had lightened completely and turned a milky blue. A barge passed and the bargee, who sported a red and white spotted scarf knotted around his throat, waved to them. They waved back and he gave them a little bow, which made them smile. It was still possible to smile, thought Natasha.

'There's the Eiffel Tower.' Eva pointed downriver. 'Your father and I went to the top and looked out over the city.' She turned the other way. 'And there's the cathedral of Notre-Dame.' She was still smiling. 'Oh, I hope we can stay here, Natasha!'

'We'll find a way.'

But how were they even to begin to make this new start? They had nowhere to live, no contacts, and not much money. Leaving Marie and Kyril on a seat by the river Natasha and her mother went to a bank on one of the fine, wide boulevards to change their roubles into francs. They seemed not to get much for their Russian money. They looked at it in dismay.

'We shall have to try to earn some,' said Eva. But none of them had ever earned anything in their lives. What could they do? 'We could work in a shop perhaps, Marie and I.'

'I could too,' said Natasha. She was tall and looked older than her age. She glanced down at her shabby clothes and then at her mother's. 'Do you think anyone would employ us dressed like this?'

Eva sighed. 'If only we knew someone who could help us just to get started. I'm sure some of our old friends must be here, somewhere in the city, if only we knew where.' Many of their friends and acquaintances had fled at the time of the revolution and Paris would have been the obvious place for them to make for since they spoke French fluently.

They spent the day on the move, roving along the boulevards and up the narrow side streets, slowing whenever they approached one of the city's numerous cafes, seeking the sight of familiar faces, listening for the sound of the Russian language. By night-time they were tired and even Natasha was low in spirit.

'We can't sleep another night on the ground,' said Marie. No one was prepared to argue.

They decided to use a little of their money to rent a room in a cheap hotel at the top of the Boulevard Saint Michel, not far from the Luxembourg Gardens. The corridors were dark and dingy and the smelly toilet at the end of the passage consisted of a hole in the ground and two places to put one's feet. But that was preferable to having to squat under a bridge.

Their room contained little furniture, only a high double bed with two dirty grey blankets, a scabby velvet chaise longue and an upright chair. Eva, Marie and Kyril slept in the bed, and Natasha on the chaise longue. The latter was not overly comfortable, but after the unyielding ground it felt inviting and Natasha dropped at once into a deep sleep.

In the morning, she got up feeling rested for the first time in days. She went out to a boulangerie to get their morning bread and it was there that she met Eugenie, who would in due course of time become the grandmother of Anna and the great-grandmother of Alex and Sonya.

The baker's shop was busy with people buying their breakfast baguettes. In the queue, in front of Natasha, there was a girl of about her own age. She had long, wavy dark hair that hung to her waist and was wearing a pretty blue dress with a deeper blue jacket over it. Her hair shone with cleanliness and her teeth, when she laughed, showed white and even. Natasha shrank back against the wall feeling grubby and shoddy. No one would imagine that once upon a time she too had worn nice clothes and had had shiny hair.

The girl was talking to another in the queue in

front of her. They were discussing an outing, a proposed picnic to a park. They were hoping the weather would stay fair. It took a moment for Natasha to register the fact that they were speaking in Russian!

The girl in blue glanced round and Natasha stammered, in that language, 'Excuse me, are you from Russia?'

'No, Paris.'

'Oh.' Natasha could not hold back her disappointment. 'You've always lived here?'

'This is where I was born. My mother is Russian, but my father was French. He's dead.' There was a catch in the girl's voice. 'He was killed in the war.'

'So was mine.' They had more than one thing in common then. 'We had to leave our home in St Petersburg because of the revolution.'

'That's where my mother was born. She came to Paris to marry my father. My mother would love to meet you, I'm sure she would.'

The girl bought her bread and waited while Natasha paid for hers. They left the shop together.

'Would you come to visit us, this afternoon perhaps? We live near by.'

Natasha said that she would love to visit them and asked if she could bring her mother and her aunt and small cousin with her, explaining that it would be difficult to leave them behind. 'Would that be all right?'

'Of course,' said the girl. She had a wide smile. 'By the way, my name is Eugénie.'

'And I am Natasha.'

TWENTY-SIX

IN PURSUIT OF PLEASURE

*A*lex jumped on his bike and pedalled at speed into the village. He must find out who had bought *A Box of Delights* at the village fête. Their future could depend on it. His father had warned him that it might be difficult. Anyone could have bought the book. And it might not necessarily have been someone in the village. Sometimes dealers from far afield came to the fair looking for bargains.

Alex went first to the manse, a good place to start when one had any query. The minister had gone to visit a sick parishioner, but Mrs Bell was in the kitchen making scones. The first batch was cooling on a wire tray and smelt delicious.

'Have one,' she invited. 'There's some of my new strawberry jam there to go with it.'

While Alex ate his scone he told her about the book.

'That could be some job to track down!' said Mrs Bell. 'Folk come from all over, as you know. Your best bet would be to go and see Mrs Crawford. She was running the book stall this year.'

Mrs Crawford lived in a house at the other end of

the street. The front door was closed. Alex knocked and waited, but nobody came. He knocked again and kicked his heels on the edge of the kerb. He couldn't stand still.

The next-door neighbour pushed up her window. 'They went out. An hour or two ago. I think they were going shopping in the town.'

'You don't know when they'll be back, I suppose?'

'Couldn't say, I'm afraid. How's Sonya? No change?' She shook her head. 'Terrible business, that. As if you hadn't enough on your plate. Troubles never come singly, so they say.'

Alex lingered. 'Did you go to the fête this year?'

The woman looked at him. Well, of course she had. A funny question that to be asking. 'You were there yourself, were you not?'

'I just wondered . . . You wouldn't have bought a copy of *A Box of Delights*, by any chance?'

'*Box of Delights*?'

'It's a book.'

'Never heard of it.'

'It's just that we gave a copy to the fête and there was a letter left inside it.'

'Oh, I see. Well, if I hear of anyone finding it, I'll let you know. What did you say it was called?' Alex repeated the title and she withdrew her head and let the window down.

He thought next of Mrs Gordon, the schoolteacher. She might have bought it for the school. He cycled along to the schoolhouse, which was next door to the two-teacher primary school. He had been a pupil there until he was twelve and Sonya had left at the end of last term, ready to go up to the secondary school in the town with him. Would she ever go there now? She didn't seem to be making any progress. For a moment he felt down, then he gave himself a shake. He had to get on with the job in hand.

This house also looked terribly shut up. It was the school holidays of course. There was still a week to go till term started. He rang the bell, but as he listened to it echoing away inside the house he had a horrible feeling he was going to strike unlucky here too. Mrs Gordon might have the copy of *A Box of Delights*, but if she did it would be behind the locked door of either the house or the school.

The postie's van came along and slowed up. 'They're away,' he called, putting his head out of the window. 'Went to Majorca yesterday. For the week.'

'Thanks,' said Alex. Then he waved to the postman and shouted, 'Hang on a minute, would you, Hamish!'

Hamish hung on. Alex ran over to the van and told him about his quest.

'I'll spread the news,' said Hamish. 'I'll ask everybody I see. And I do see everybody most days in the week.'

He took off.

The shop, thought Alex. That was another place where news spread like wildfire, too much so at times.

'Why don't you put a notice up on the board?' suggested Mrs Robertson. 'Everybody that comes in reads the board. Here's a postcard for you to write it on.'

Alex took the plain white postcard to the post-office counter and wrote the message with the post-office pen that was attached by a cord to the wall.

'Would anyone who bought *A Box of Delights* by John Masefield at the village fête in June or who knows of anyone who did, please get in touch with either Duncan or Alex McKinnon.' He printed their phone number at the bottom.

He pinned the card to the board, alongside all the others advertising joinery and plumbing services, cottages for rent, and goods for sale, which ranged from loads of hardwood logs to push-chairs, second-hand gardening tools and electric cookers.

As he was leaving the shop the Crawfords' car went by. Alex raced along the street after it. The Crawfords stopped in front of their door and Mrs Crawford got out of the passenger side.

'Mrs Crawford,' panted Alex, 'could I speak to you for a moment?' When he had recovered his breath he said, 'It's about the village fête. The book stall. You wouldn't happen to remember who bought *A Box of Delights*, would you?'

'Why yes, I would,' she said with a smile. 'I did. For my grandson. He's just seven, but he loves books. You've met Rory, haven't you?'

'Oh, yes, yes I have. Where is it that he lives?' Not in the village, anyway, Alex knew that.

'Edinburgh.'

'Edinburgh?'

'Why yes. Anything the matter, Alex?'

'Well, we're not sure, but there *might* be a note in the book, an important note. Do you think you could ring them up and ask them to look?'

'I don't have to do that. I haven't given it to Rory yet, I was waiting till he came up to visit us.'

'So you've still got it?'

'I have. Come on in and I'll find it.'

Alex followed her into the living room.

'Now where did I put it?' She frowned. 'I believe Malcolm was looking at it. Malcolm,' Mrs Crawford called to her husband, who was coming into the hall now, 'do you know where that copy of *A Box of Delights* is that I bought at the fête?'

Mr Crawford had a carton of groceries in his arms. 'I've been reading it. Enjoying it too. Hang on a minute till I get rid of this lot.' He took the carton into the kitchen and then came back. 'It should be beside my chair.' He reached down beside one of the armchairs. 'Here it is!' He presented Alex with the book.

Alex flicked excitedly through the pages, his heart racing. He couldn't find anything. He went through it again.

'It's not there!' he cried.

'He's looking for a note, Malcolm,' explained Mrs Crawford. 'You didn't find any bits of paper in it, did you?'

'Well, actually, I did. There was a piece of paper with a couple of lines scrawled on it. Didn't make much sense. I threw it away, I'm afraid. I hope it wasn't important?'

TWENTY-SEVEN

PARIS, 1919
THE BEGINNING OF A LONG FRIENDSHIP

*E*ugénie lived with her mother Vera in an airy, spacious flat overlooking the Luxembourg Gardens. Vera welcomed them and over coffee and cake she and Eva soon discovered that they had had friends in common in St Petersburg. When she found that they had nowhere to live she immediately offered them the use of two of their spare rooms. 'We have a lot of extra space and now there is only Eugénie and I.'

The two women became firm friends, as did their daughters. Eugénie gave Natasha a couple of her dresses, insisting that she take them, and Vera passed on some of her clothes to Eva and Marie. They were in such need of them that they accepted gratefully. They threw their rags away.

'We won't impose on you for ever, Vera,' said Eva. 'We'll stay only until we manage to get back on our feet.' What she didn't know is that she would stay until she died, and Natasha until she married Alasdair Fleming and went to live in Scotland.

Vera's husband had been a financier, whose money had been invested in a Swiss bank. He had therefore left his widow comfortably off.

'We are not short of money,' Vera told Eva.

'But we can't let you keep us,' Eva protested.

'You mustn't let it worry you.'

But it did worry Eva, and Natasha too. They discussed the problem in the privacy of their room.

'We shall have to find some means of earning our living,' said Eva. 'Perhaps Marie and I could do some sewing. Marie is a fine needlewoman and although I'm not as good as she is, I'm not too bad. I think I would enjoy using patterns and cutting out.'

The women had done embroidery mostly, although Marie had made a few christening gowns, including the ones that Natasha and Kyril had worn. They had been sad to leave those behind. But then they had had to leave so much behind.

To begin with, Marie said, 'Go into *business*? We don't know anything about such things.'

'We shall learn,' said Eva. 'And Natasha will help us. She has a good head on her.'

Marie continued to protest and express doubts, but they could see that she was becoming interested. Eventually she said, 'I suppose we have no choice?'

'None,' said Eva firmly, who wanted to waste no more time.

'Unless you would rather scrub floors,' said Natasha, a little wickedly. 'The cafe on the corner is looking for a cleaner.'

They went ahead and set themselves up in the dressmaking business. A lot of women needed to replenish their wardrobes after the war. They would offer favourable rates.

Their first customer was Russian – a large number of émigrés were living in Paris – and a friend of Vera's.

She ordered an afternoon dress. She was delighted with the result and went on to order a suit. Then she sent her daughter along to have an evening dress made. After that came a friend of the daughter who, having seen the dress, decided that she would like to have one made for herself. And so it went on. The business grew by word of mouth and gradually the women were able to support themselves.

Natasha joined Eugénie at her school. They walked there together daily, sat next to each other in class, were seldom apart. They liked the same things and quarrelled but rarely. When they finished school they went to university, commencing at the same time, Eugénie to study music, Natasha to study medicine. The girls were of the same height and build and could have been twins, except that Natasha was fair and Eugénie dark. Everyone commented on their closeness. It was thought that nothing could separate them.

Eugénie married before Natasha. Pierre was a violinist, quite a brilliant one. Natasha was chief bridesmaid at the wedding. A year later, Eugénie gave birth to a daughter. Natasha was godmother.

And then Natasha met a Scotsman, Alasdair Fleming, when he was on holiday in Paris. They fell in love and six months later, decided to marry. Eugénie was appalled. 'You can't go and live in Scotland!' But Natasha had already taken the decision to do so.

The night before their wedding, Alasdair arrived bringing with him a surprise present for Natasha. He said he had bought it at an auction in London.

'What can it be?' Natasha held the object in her hands. It was rectangular, about forty centimetres across, wrapped in gold and white paper, and it felt like a box.

'Go on, open it!' Alasdair was smiling. He could barely contain his excitement.

Carefully, she unwrapped the parcel. She was so surprised she almost dropped it.

'It's my sewing basket!' she cried, raising the lid and looking inside. She couldn't believe it! Everything looked just as she had left it. The silken threads, the packet of needles, the little silver scissors. She lifted them out and held them in her hand.

'I was fairly sure it must be yours,' said Alasdair. 'You had described it to me. I had such a strange feeling when my eye lit on the basket, as if I had seen it before. And your name "Natasha" was embroidered on the inside of the lid.'

Natasha felt as if a part of her childhood had been returned to her. It brought back memories of sitting in her sunlit room with the box in her lap and the window open, letting in the smell of spring air and the sound of bargees on the river Neva calling to one another.

An exile, they concluded, must have brought the basket from St Petersburg to London. It was possible that someone, perhaps their former maid Lena, had sold it in the first instance.

'It's a magic box,' said Alasdair.

'A magic box?'

'Yes, didn't you know?'

Natasha shook her head.

'The auctioneer told me about it. He had come across a similar box before. Watch!' Alasdair lifted the lid and putting his thumbs into the bottom far corners of the basket, he pressed down firmly. Slowly, a small tray slid out from underneath.

Natasha was overwhelmed. 'A secret tray! How wonderful! I won't tell anyone else. Only you and I will know. I'll be able to keep secret things in there.' She had always liked secrets.

And so Natasha went to live with Alasdair in Scotland, taking her sewing basket with her. They lived in a house on the west coast looking over a long sea loch. Some years later, Anna, the granddaughter of Eugénie, met Duncan McKinnon on a visit to Natasha, and fell in love with him. And so she too came to live in Argyll, and they had two children, Alexander and Sonya, who Natasha looked upon as her own great-grandchildren.

TWENTY-EIGHT

THE OTHER BOX OF DELIGHTS

'Do you think you could remember what was in the note?' asked Alex anxiously. To think that they had come this far and the last clue had been thrown away!

Mr Crawford thought. 'It was something about another box of delights.' He shrugged. 'But beyond that I can't really remember. I'm very sorry, but I only gave it a quick glance. If only I'd known it was important!'

'But it did say something else apart from "a box of delights", did it?' asked Alex anxiously.

'I'm pretty certain it did. I think it was some sort of instruction.'

'About doing something? Looking for something?'

'Could have been. My memory isn't as good as it used to be, I'm afraid. Old age, you know!'

'Would you like to have the book back, Alex?' asked Mrs Crawford.

'No, thanks all the same. It was only the piece of paper that I wanted.'

Only! Alex cycled home feeling pent up with frustration. He dropped his bicycle on the front step and ran in to tell his father about this latest turn of events.

'Imagine, Mr Crawford *threw away* our very last clue!'

'We do know part of it,' Duncan reminded him.

'Another box of delights. It can't be another book, can it? Natasha said it was the last clue.'

'So it should lead us to the will itself.'

'And she wouldn't put that inside a book, would she?'

But how did they know how Natasha's mind would have been working at that stage?

'If only Mr Crawford had remembered the other part!' said Alex gloomily. After all the excitement of the search he felt down in the dumps. 'It's not worth looking at other books, is it?' But he needed to do something. He couldn't just sit here hoping Mr Crawford would have a sudden flash of recall and ring up and say, 'I've just remembered!'

'Why don't you go up to Natasha's room and look at some of her boxes?' suggested Duncan. 'Any kind of box. She had quite a number, didn't she?'

They had already searched Natasha's room more than once, but Alex agreed to give it another try. It was possible that they might have missed something, though not very likely. He investigated every box he could find, inside and out. He was thorough. He went through jewellery boxes and trinket boxes, and two hat boxes that contained the summery kind of hats with long trailing ribbons that Natasha had liked to wear in the garden, and old shoe boxes full of photographs. But there was no sign of a will or of any kind of paper in any of the boxes. Alex returned to the library and flung himself down in the big leather chair where Natasha herself used to sit reading.

'When your mother phones we'll ask her,' said Duncan. 'She might have an idea of what kind of box Natasha might have meant.'

Anna was later ringing that day than usual. Alex couldn't stay still. He got up and wandered restlessly round the house; his father occupied himself in the kitchen making a chicken casserole. When the phone did ring Alex made a dash for it.

'Hi, Mum!' He asked first after Sonya.

'She seems to me to be going through a change. I can't explain exactly. The nurse doesn't see it. But I feel the expression on her face looks different.'

They talked for a moment about Sonya, with Duncan coming in on the extension, and then Alex asked his question. 'Mum, what would Natasha mean by a box of delights? Other than the book?'

'Why, her sewing basket!' said Anna. 'She always said just to look at it delighted her. Especially because of Alasdair finding it at that auction in London. She said it was like a miracle that it should turn up all those years later and he should be the one to buy it.'

'But we've already looked in the sewing basket,' said Alex. 'Dozens of times. Sonya too. She opened that basket nearly every day after Natasha died. She kept all sorts of things in it. How could she possibly have missed a piece of paper?'

'It is a bit of a mystery,' agreed his mother. 'Why don't you go and take just one final look?'

'Oh, all right.'

Alex was sure it was going to be a waste of time, but he went off to do it, leaving his father on the line.

He opened the basket, looked inside took out the threads and the packets of needles and pins, and the little pair of silver scissors. He ran his fingers over the satin covering and the satin lining. He examined the lid, the sides, the bottom. He closed the lid, feeling utterly frustrated. Perhaps Natasha had put the will in there originally, but it had got mislaid. Perhaps she had never put it in there. Perhaps she had been playing games with them all along.

TWENTY-NINE

SONYA'S DREAM

*S*onya was dreaming. She was in that state of consciousness when she knew she was dreaming. It was as if she was above what was going on, and observing it. Natasha was in the dream, not the Natasha that Sonya had known with white hair and a slight stoop to her back. This was a younger version of Natasha with a straight back and loose fair hair, yet Sonya recognized her . . .

Natasha is in a sunlit room with Alasdair, holding something between her hands. It is a present, which he tells her he bought at an auction in London. She is laughing and asking, 'What can it be?' And Alasdair is saying, 'It's a surprise. Go on, Natasha, open it!' She carefully takes off the gold and white paper. Her eyes widen as she sees what it is, as if she cannot believe what she is seeing.

'It's my sewing basket!' she cries, laughing and crying at the same time.

'I was pretty sure it must be. I saw your name embroidered on the lid!'

She tells him that it is the best present he could ever

have given her. He has brought back a part of her childhood for her.

'It's a magic box,' says Alasdair. He too is smiling.

'Magic?'

'Yes, didn't you know?'

She shakes her head.

'The auctioneer told me about it. He had come across a similar box before. Watch!' Alasdair lifts the lid and putting his thumbs into the bottom far corners of the basket, presses down. Slowly, a shallow tray slides out from underneath.

Natasha is overwhelmed. 'A secret tray! How wonderful! I won't tell anyone else. Only you and I will know. I'll be able to keep secret things in there.' She likes secrets . . .

Sonya felt herself surfacing. It was like being at the bottom of the ocean bed and gradually coming up to the top. She was still holding on to the dream, she could still see Natasha's smiling face as she bent over the sewing basket. She told herself to hold on to the dream, not to let it go, and to remember. She knew that it was important to remember. *Remember, remember . . .* She was going up and up. She was reaching the surface. She opened her eyes and the light burst upon her.

'Sonya!'

She heard her name, recognized the voice. She blinked. The light was so powerful that she almost could not bear it. She wanted to close her eyes again and sink back down into that other world. What was that other world? What had she been dreaming about? She frowned. She remembered that she had been dreaming, but she could not remember what it was that she had dreamt. Yet she knew it was important to remember.

'Sonya, it's Mum here. Can you hear me?'

Sonya looked up into the face bending over hers. She knew it. She knew it well. 'Hello, Mum,' she said. Her voice felt strange and creaky as it emerged.

'Oh, darling, I can't believe it!' Her mother was crying.

'Where am I?' asked Sonya. She did not recognize the room or the woman who was standing at the other side of the bed wearing a white apron. Then she thought, She's a nurse, isn't she? Yes, of course she is. I've seen a nurse before.

'You had an accident, Sonya,' said her mother.

'An accident?' Sonya had no memory of that.

'You've been sleeping.'

'How long?'

'Quite long. Days.'

'*Days?*'

'Weeks. Five, almost six.'

Sonya could not comprehend that either.

'Don't think about it,' said her mother. 'Just rest. I'm going to leave you with the nurse while I go and phone Dad and Alex.'

'Alex?'

'You remember Alex, don't you? Your brother?'

Sonya nodded. Yes, she remembered her brother with his dark eyes and serious frown. Things were gradually coming back to her. Some things, at least.

A doctor came and examined her and removed a tube that he said had been feeding her.

'Have I not been eating?'

'You couldn't eat while you were asleep, could you?' He smiled. Everyone was smiling at her. The doctor said she could have some weak tea and toast. The nurse brought it and helped her to sit up. Her mother held the cup. Sonya's own hands and arms felt too weak to hold it herself. It would take a little while for her to get her strength back, said the nurse. Her muscles would have weakened from lying so long in bed.

'But you're young. It won't be long before you're strong again.'

'And then you'll be able to come home,' said Anna.

THIRTY

THE RETURN VISIT OF BORIS MALENKOV AND
MR HATTON-FLITCH

Sonya would not be allowed to come home for some time. She must stay in hospital until she became stronger. They thought that her brain had suffered no permanent damage, although she was still having headaches and she kept forgetting things that she thought she should know. She felt at times that she was chasing them round the edges of her brain, but they kept scurrying away out of her grasp. The doctors said she shouldn't let it worry her, it was a case of letting everything return gradually to a state of normality. She couldn't expect to emerge from a coma and jump out of bed the next day!

Mr Bell, the minister, drove Alex and Duncan down to Glasgow. They thought Sonya looked thin and pale, but that was not surprising. Anna looked rather pale and thin too. Sonya had the same wide smile though, and her eyes lit up when she saw them. She was sitting in an armchair by the window. She got up to hug them and all their eyes were damp.

'Mrs Bell sent you one of her carrot cakes,' said Alex, putting it on the bedside table, 'and a batch of her scones. She says we've got to fatten you up.'

Sonya laughed. 'What's been happening in the village? Tell me all the news! I want to hear everything. How's Tobias?'

'He's great,' said Alex. 'He says you're to hurry home and get on his back again.'

'Tell him I'll be there as soon as they let me out of here. I'm dying to get home!'

They had decided not to mention the missing will and Cousin Boris and it seemed that she had forgotten them.

They didn't stay too long. After an hour they could see that Sonya was wilting.

'See you back home then!' said Alex. 'So stay out of trouble until then, Sis, OK?'

'OK.' She gave him a weak punch in the chest.

The phone was ringing as they opened the front door on their return. Alex ran ahead to answer it. It was Boris on the line. He had been phoning at regular intervals to find out if there was any change in Sonya's condition. On hearing the latest news, he declared himself delighted. He then did a bit of throat-clearing and said, half apologetically, that he would be coming north with Mr Hatton-Flitch in two weeks' time.

'Oh?' said Alex.

'Well, yes, we expect to get confirmation from the court then.'

'We've only got two weeks,' said Alex to his father, after he'd put the receiver down.

He was determined to carry on his search for the will, even though it was beginning to seem more and more like a wild goose chase. He took down every book from the shelves in the library and went through them, on the off-chance that Natasha might have tucked away an extra clue. But she hadn't. And it took hours.

He went back to school. The doctors were pleased with Sonya's progress and had promised her that soon she would be able to go home. And soon Cousin Boris and his lawyer would be getting into their black car and heading north.

'We have to face up to it,' said Duncan. 'We're going to have to start looking for somewhere else to live.'

Mr Trotter had sent details of two or three country houses within a fifty mile radius, but they were too far away from their school to begin with, and to be going on with, they couldn't afford them. The trouble with most local properties was that they were rented out as holiday lets during the season, which gave their owners a higher return. The summer rents would be too expensive for the McKinnons. They also had the complication that not every house would be suitable for Duncan with his wheelchair.

'Boris couldn't put us out in the road, could he?' said Alex.

'We could stall for a while, but eventually we'd have to go. I'd rather we went in a dignified way and found our own accommodation,' said Duncan.

Alex didn't feel at all dignified about the idea of giving up their home! He kicked a burst football along the beach, pretending it was Boris's head! At least Sonya was growing stronger day by day. And as his father said, that was more important than anything else that was happening to them.

Mr Hatton-Flitch telephoned. 'Mr Malenkov has kindly offered to pay a rental for you for the first three months. Mr Trotter has a house on his books that might suit.'

The house he proposed would not suit. It was one that Mr Trotter had already offered them. After the first three months they would not be able to afford the rent. And they didn't want to accept any favours from Boris.

'Mr Malenkov might be prepared to extend his offer to six months,' said Mr Hatton-Flitch.

Anything to get them out, thought Alex. His father turned that offer down as well.

The minister came up to tell them that Mrs McPherson, one of the villagers, was prepared to rent them a cottage which he thought might suit them. The rent was reasonable. He drove them down to the village to look at it. Mrs McPherson had given him the key.

Birch Cottage sat straight on to the pavement like the other village houses, with a small back garden. The doorway and hall were wide enough for Duncan's chair. That was the first hurdle satisfactorily crossed.

The sitting room proved to be small, but bright enough, as was the bedroom off the hall on the other side. At the back was a large kitchen, big enough to eat in, and a decent-sized bathroom. Upstairs were two attic bedrooms, which would do for Alex and Sonya. Duncan would be able to live totally on the ground floor.

'I think we'll have to take it,' he said.

'I'll tell Mrs McPherson,' said Mr Bell.

Two days later, Sonya came home. They didn't tell her that day about their forthcoming move, but they couldn't keep it from her for long. She was very upset, as they had expected.

'We've got to leave here?' She frowned. 'But wasn't there a will? Natasha said she'd made one.'

'We couldn't find it,' said Alex. 'We've looked everywhere.' He told her about the hunt and the trail they'd followed. 'I think Natasha may just have played a game with us.'

'She wouldn't do that. Not with something so serious. She really did want us to have the house, I know she did!'

'Don't get worked up now, love.' Her mother put her arm round Sonya. 'It won't do you any good. We'll have to go. We have no choice. So we must be brave about it.'

'I don't want to be brave!' Sonya dissolved into a torrent of tears.

Alex went back to kicking the burst football along the beach. And when he'd had enough of that he went and talked to Tobias, which always calmed him.

Cousin Boris and Mr Hatton-Flitch arrived on the day before their claim was due to be confirmed at the sheriff court. They had phoned to say they would call in on them, just to go over a few details. They came in their long, sleek black car.

As soon as Sonya saw it turning in at the drive she went up to her room. The sight of it had brought back in a rush the memory of running across the lawn towards it. And then, nothing. Just a blank. Blackness.

She went to her desk where her sewing basket lay. She touched the lid. This beautiful old box had often comforted her when she was down. And she was down now. She opened the lid and took out the little jewelled thimble that Natasha had given her. Natasha had always said it would bring her luck. 'Never let it go,' she had told her.

The door opened and Alex put his head round. 'What are you up to?'

'Nothing.' Sonya shrugged. Whenever she disappeared on her own for a few minutes they came to see if she was all right. They were anxious about her. But she was getting better. The headaches were lessening and her mind felt clearer.

Alex came in and sat on the edge of the bed. 'We'll be OK, Sis, you'll see.'

'I expect we will. But I *know* Natasha wanted us to go on living here. It just doesn't seem right.' Sonya lifted a packet of needles from the basket and took one out. She frowned and racked her brains. She felt as if she were on the brink of remembering something, something to do with Natasha, but it kept sliding away from the edge of her mind. It was quite infuriating every time this happened. Idly she tested the point of the needle against her thumb, trying to recall what it was that she wanted to recall.

'Careful, Sis,' said Alex. 'Watch what you're doing.'

Sonya's hand slipped and the point of the needle plunged straight into the soft flesh of her palm, making her cry out.

'Are you all right?' Alex leapt off the bed.

'Alex, Alex!' Sonya cried. Blood was dripping from her hand. 'I've remembered, I've remembered!'

'Remembered what?'

'The secret drawer. Alasdair showed it to Natasha. It's at the bottom of the basket!'

'The bottom of the basket? It can't be. I've looked.'

'Wait! Give me some of those tissues, would you?'

Alex passed them over and she wrapped them round the palm of her left hand to staunch the bleeding. With her other hand she removed the contents of the sewing basket. Then she put both thumbs into the bottom far corners of the box and pressed hard. She held her breath.

Slowly a shallow tray came sliding out from underneath the basket. Alex gasped. Lying on the tray was a single sheet of strong white paper.

THIRTY-ONE

NATASHA'S WILL

*S*onya lifted up the paper with trembling hands and read it aloud.

'This is my last will and testament. I hereby bequeath my estate and all my possessions to Anna McKinnon, granddaughter of my dear friend Eugénie, and to her husband, Duncan. In due course this estate should pass to her children, Alexander McKinnon and Sonya McKinnon. It is my greatest wish that the McKinnon family should live on in this house and enjoy it.'

The will was signed 'Natasha Fleming, née Denisova,' and had been witnessed by Morag and Alan Forsyth, two old friends of Natasha's and Alasdair's, who had lived in the village. Alan had died shortly before Natasha, and his wife a few days afterwards, unexpectedly of a heart attack. The main signature was vigorous and undisputedly Natasha's.

Sonya and Alex laughed and hugged each other.

'Don't crush the will!' cried Sonya. 'Let's go and show it to Mum and Dad.'

'And Mr Hatton-Flitch! And Cousin Boris!'

They ran downstairs shouting, 'Mum! Dad! We've found it!'

Their parents were in the hall below with the two visitors. They stood in front of the grandfather clock and looked as if they were locked in dispute. Anna had said she was determined to fight to keep the clock.

'Found what?' asked Duncan.

'The will!' cried Sonya. 'We've found the will!'

Boris blenched. 'The will? You can't have found it.'

'We have! Look, here it is! The house is ours! Natasha has left it to *us*.'

Mr Hatton-Flitch's eyes were almost popping out of his head. 'May I see, please?' He tried to take the paper, but Sonya whirled past him and gave it to her mother.

'Look, Mum, it says that Natasha has left the house to you and Dad. And *all* her possessions. That would mean the clock as well. Everything!'

'There must be some mistake,' said Boris, his voice on the verge of cracking. 'This piece of paper can't possibly be valid, can it, Mr Hatton-Flitch? It's not a proper will, surely?'

The lawyer was permitted to see the paper, although Anna kept a firm hold of it. He put on his gold-rimmed spectacles to read it and his face also changed colour visibly. 'I'm afraid it looks valid, Mr Malenkov. It quite clearly sets out Mrs Natasha Fleming's intentions. We shall have to get the signature verified, of course, but if it is genuine –'

Anna interrupted him. 'It's genuine. You can take my word for that. But you're welcome to have it verified, of course. I shall be taking it straight away to our lawyer so that he can establish our claim.'

'I shall challenge it,' declared Boris, straightening

166

himself up. 'I am Natasha's only known surviving relative.'

'I doubt if I would advise it,' said Mr Hatton-Flitch. 'Not if the signature is valid.'

Sonya and Alex smiled at each other.

Mr Hatton-Flitch and Mr Boris Malenkov took off soon afterwards in their long sleek black car and were never seen or heard of in that part of the world again.

There was general rejoicing in the village and for miles around. The McKinnons gave a splendid party, to which more than a hundred people came. They strung fairy lights across the garden and a local trio played traditional Scottish and Russian music and they danced under the stars until midnight.

And so Natasha's greatest wish came true: that the McKinnons should live on in the house by the loch and enjoy it.